THE PROTESTER HAS BEEN RELEASED

stories and a novella

Janet Sarbanes

C&R Press
Conscious & Responsible

Cover art: Other Side by Eugenia Loli
Interior design by C&R Press
Exterior design by C&R Press

Copyright ©2016 by Janet Sarbanes

Library of Congress Cataloging-in-Publication Data

ISBN: 978-1-936196-65-4
LCCN: 2016952190

C&R Press
Conscious & Responsible
www.crpress.org
Winston-Salem, North Carolina

For special discounted bulk purchases, please contact:
C&R Press sales@crpress.org
Contact lharms@crpress.org to book events, readings and author signings.

For Ken, my love
and
Lena, my light

Table of Contents

Laika Hears the Music of the Spheres

It's over now, the terrible heat. The terrible heat and the horrible noise have passed. I can hear my heart beating, fast then not so fast. Soon He will come to let me out. This is my favorite time, when all is still and quiet, and He is coming.

I have to sit like this a lot, sometimes they make me sit for days, but I like to sit. I listen to my breath moving in and out, and forget that I'm hungry, or hot, or thirsty; that I can't stand or turn around. I forget about Him even, my longing for Him, though it was He who taught me how to find this peace.

But something's different today. Though my heart has calmed, I feel strange. Strange and light. Even though I can't move, trapped as I am between two pillows in my suit—still, I'm rising. If I weren't so firmly tethered, I might float away. Everything else is the same as always, but this is different.

***

Something's wrong. He hasn't come to let me out. I search my memory for clues. I think it was yesterday morning, or perhaps the day before, that He took down the Leash and opened the Cage. "Walk? Walk?" He asked, in that simple way of His.

"Yes, of course!" I responded happily. "Shall we go somewhere special, like the Beach?" But He ignored my question, or perhaps He simply didn't understand. After all this time, I know so many of His words and He knows so few of mine.

We did go to the Beach, down to the Great Water, but He wouldn't let me go in, only stand at the edge and smell the salt. There were many gorgeous smells on the Beach that day, even some dead things, but He wouldn't let me near them. "Sit, Laika," He said, and I sat.

He stroked my head with His heavy hand, looking out at the Great Water. I was happy, as I always am sitting next to Him. No matter what I have to endure, when He comes to let me out again, I'm happy.

He tried to tell me something, but they weren't the words I know. They were the words they use when talking across their desks or walking down the corridors. The only one I recognized was "Limonchik," the name no other calls me. *Limonchik*, He kept saying over and over, putting that word up against the other ones, as if it could somehow make them mean something to me, or make me mean something to those words. Whatever He was saying, it caused warm water to stream from his eyes and His body to jerk and tremble.

"Oh come on, it can't be that bad," I said to Him. He laughed and took hold of the paw I had proffered, but the water continued to leak from His eyes.

***

Something's definitely wrong. I know this from the floating feeling I have, and the fact that He does not come. I'm ravenous, too; usually they don't let me get this hungry. And the thirst, I sit and try to forget the thirst.

***

There's a horrible creature in here with me. She's only just made herself known. She bites me constantly and says terrible things.

"Ouch!" I yelp. "How did you get in here?"

"I'm a flea. We get in everywhere."

"But they wash me once a week. With a special shampoo."

"Oh yes. They treat you so nice."

"Because I'm not a dirty parasite. Ouch! Stop biting me!"

"I can't," she says. "I'm a dirty parasite."

***

The Flea is very angry to be stuck in here with me. I think she bites me more than she has to. "We'll be out soon," I tell her, despite my doubts. "He's going to come."

But the Flea will have none of it. And she has a peculiar explanation for what I'm feeling. She says we are, in fact, floating. "And where we're floating, no one has ever floated before."

"Nonsense! This a Test. I've been through loads of them."

"And what did you think they were testing for?"

I ponder her question long and hard, even though she's biting me.

"They were testing my loyalty," I say finally.

"Your loyalty? Your loyalty to whom?"

"To Him."

"To Him? They don't need to test your loyalty to Him. You're a *dog*."

***

But she's wrong, this flea. I wasn't always so loyal. When they first caught me and brought me in off the streets, I wouldn't let them near. I bit one of them, hard. When he screamed, I bared my bloody fangs and laughed. I paced my cage, I gnawed at the bars, I plotted my escape. I cursed them—long, elaborate curses, and though they understood nothing, my enmity chilled them. "*Volchishka*," they called me, Little Wolf, and tried to win me over with meaty bones. But I knew that the key to freedom is to live for something other than food.

They were ready to turn me out: ungrateful little bitch, unlovable, untouchable, untrainable, and I was more than ready to go. But then one day He came, in a white coat just like the rest of them, though on him it seemed less a hygienic precaution than the outer manifestation of an inner purity.

"*Limonchik*," he chuckled when he saw my sour face. Little Lemon. "She's just what we want—a fighter." He offered me nothing but a simple command: "Sit, Laika."

And I sat.

***

I think the Flea is right. I've been peering through my window at a deep dark night. The window's small and round, but large enough to tell: it never ends.

***

The Flea has been feeding me more of her peculiar ideas. I'm on a mission, apparently, but my mission has nothing to do with the one who calls me *Limonchik*, or only so much as He is one of them, the men who've sent me into the deep dark night that never ends. They want to go there too someday, and they need to know if they will survive the trip.

"But why would they want to go where their survival is threatened?" I ask.

"Because they feel trapped."

"Trapped? By what?"

"By their tiny planet, which is no more than a plaything in the hands of the Universe, a bright blue ball. They want to know if there are other worlds out there—other planets they could live on."

"And are there other worlds?"

"That's what they must find out, before the Americans do."

***

The Americans are another band of men shooting small animals into the deep dark night. Whoever finds the other worlds first, the Flea tells me, will blow up Earth and move on.

"But why?"

"Because they can. Don't you know enough of Man to know that what I say is true?"

"Not my Man," I answer silently, for what does a flea know of higher motives? Not Him.

***

I think I'm starting to understand this mission. Not the race with the Americans, that seems childish to me, but the desire to know what's out there. What I've glimpsed through my porthole is so impossibly beautiful—there are no words to describe it. I think He must have been the one who put in the window. He was the one who wanted me to see.

***

I'm dizzy with hunger. In all my years of privation, there was only one other time I remember feeling like this: it was the dead of winter and there was no food left in Moscow, for man or dog. Only the fleas, those dirty parasites, continued to feast. Weak from hunger and cold, unable to go one step further, I lay down in a back alley and waited for the snow to cover me.

But it turned out I wasn't alone. A human mother was crouched there too, with her children. She looked up and watched me warily for a moment, then shoved a metal bowl in my direction. I saw the hunger in her eyes and in her children's eyes as it skittered across the ice, yet she shoved the shining bowl toward me and watched me gobble up the slop that remained. That's when I realized there's something good in them that mirrors the something good in us—something a lower order creature like the Flea could never understand.

***

I ask the Flea what it smells like out there in the deep dark night that never ends.

"Seared steak," she whispers in my ear.

***

The Flea has stopped biting me—she says I'm starving. What's more, they know I'm starving. No animal can go this long without food. They know I'm starving, that my water has run out, and still He doesn't come.

Since the Flea has stopped biting me, she will soon be starving too.

"So, you're a higher order creature after all," I say.

"No, I'm still a lower order creature," she assures me. "You just don't taste good anymore."

***

And now the Flea is dead, though not of natural causes. I killed her. It was an accident, a reflex response to a horrible thing she said—I smashed her into the wall with my shoulder—but she shouldn't have tried me. I'm in a very sensitive state.

First she told me they have no way of getting me back. They were in too much of a hurry to figure it out—it is a race, after all. That's why the warm water burst from His eyes. That was the force beyond His control. Then she said, "But He had you there, at the Beach. He could've let you go."

***

My heart beats irregularly; it stutters and stops, stutters and stops. Is he tracking this, down there on his tiny planet? Is he sorry?

I have no regrets. I loved well. I was a good dog. I untether my thoughts and let them float away; I close my eyes and fix my gaze on the bright blue ball in my mind. I sit and breathe as I've done so many times before—perhaps this is what I was training for all along. The voice in my head has at last gone silent, and I can hear the music of the spheres.

Coyoacan

They arrived in the middle of a great storm, the American, her husband and their little boy with the goggly eyes. We'd left the door to the courtyard open for them, but the front door was sandbagged so we motioned for them to come round to the kitchen. They just stood there staring at us through the window with water streaming down their faces, refusing to move. Finally, Luis pulled back some of the sandbags and pushed the door open a little. "Go around to the side please, Señor," he said to the husband, but the man jammed his way through with the stroller and she slipped in behind him, the first of many misunderstandings.

Or no, the second. It was our boss, Doña Morales, who first led them astray. I heard her speaking to the husband on the phone, telling him it was okay, all utilities on and no flooding in our neighborhood—did he think they would let the street flood so close to the house of Frida Kahlo? She told him Luis would drive them to get groceries and I would clean for them and take care of the baby while his wife did her writing and he was closing down the regional office for the company. Maybe it was his poor Spanish, maybe he wanted to believe, but they came to Coyoacan just as everyone else was leaving.

Doña Morales told us she was going, as she does every summer, to her daughter's house in Los Angeles. But why then did she empty the safe, why was she looking through the family papers the night

before she left? Why hasn't she called, as she always does, all summer
long, for updates on the tenants and to give us things to do, repairs
to make and projects to undertake? Last summer, she made us scrub
the cupboards with bleach and build fires to air the linen—which it's
true was never dry. Not that I wish to hear from her. This summer,
with all the holes in the roof and the toilets and bathtubs backing
up every other day, with the cats getting washed away, with our own
children thankfully out of the city in Veracruz—Luis's in Pachuca
with his wife, and my two girls in Papantla with my mother—but still
so far away, we have other things besides pillowcases on our minds.

We got to Mrs. Morales's house in the middle of a terrible storm, after
having spent hours in a taxi crawling through flooded streets. When
we knocked on the door, it took forever for anyone to come, and
when they finally did, the housekeeper and the chauffeur, Dolores
and Luis, they just stood at the window and waved us away. Dan had
to be quite forceful when they finally did crack the door open. It was
midnight by then and with the baby still up and us stranded there on
the porch with all of our luggage in the middle of a downpour—we
weren't about to just go away!

This morning the rain has stopped and we pad about the house in
our slippers, getting to know it. It's a glass and steel-beamed affair,
with beautiful grey-blue terrazzo floors and an atrium at the center
of the two stories, topped by a skylight. Sliding glass doors, heavi-
ly sandbagged, open onto a patio in the back; there's a serviceable
kitchen with a countertop bar, and a spacious master bedroom and
bathroom with a claw foot tub that sits under another skylight. Being
so close to Kahlo's house—right around the corner!—the landlady
has decorated in kind; the bathroom is lined with little *retablo* paintings in heavy wooden frames beseeching miracles for the sick and
maimed.

Ash will sleep in the TV room across the landing from the master
bedroom—a bit far from us for my taste, but he slept through most
of last night, waking only once to nurse. I hadn't realized this from

the photos—and Dan hadn't either—but the house is in a walled compound (as are most of the houses in Mexico City, you can't see into or out of them from the street), where the housekeeper and the chauffeur each has a room in a little outbuilding, and share a bathroom next to the laundry. They seem to cook in their rooms, but we all share the refrigerator in the kitchen.

Dolores came in to get some things as we were eating breakfast at the counter, with Ash toddling around our stools. When she smiled and spoke to him in Spanish, he froze on his wobbly legs, slack-jawed with astonishment. Dan started to ask her about setting up a childcare arrangement for me, as the landlady had promised, but I elbowed him and said not yet, let's get acquainted first. So he spoke to her for a little while in his halting Spanish, which I could somewhat understand, though I had no idea what she answered back—to me it was just a gush of bright sound. Now I wish I'd spent more time with my language CDs.

One phrase I did learn that I'm sure I'll be using a lot this summer: *mucha lluvia*. It started up again this afternoon, a hurling rain that comes at the house sideways, lancing through the cracks and pooling at the doors and windows. At lunchtime we tried to go out to a restaurant but didn't make it past the heavy wooden door to the compound. No sooner had we unlocked it and stepped over the metal frame, holding an umbrella over Ash's stroller, than a truck drove by, drenching us all, and the wind tore the umbrella from my hand. So we picked up the stroller, holding it up at both ends like a little stretcher, and ran Ash screaming back into the house. Then we raided the probiotic drink supply in the fridge—not sure if they're the housekeeper's or the chauffeur's (today is Saturday and they seem to have disappeared)—and later on, filched some eggs and tortillas for dinner. We'll replenish everything as soon as we can get a ride to the market.

The Americans are angry that we left for the weekend. They had no food in the house, and the rain, they say, made it impossible for them to go anywhere. We don't tell them where we were, in Veracruz, because Doña Morales would never let us take her car to Veracruz, but the buses no longer run to our villages and I hadn't seen my girls for so long! We were told the road was getting harder and harder to pass and the government would soon be closing it, so we took the chance. Who knows when we'll be able to go back?

To be honest, I wish I had never gone, because now I know things are no different in Veracruz. Two months of nonstop rain have taken their toll there, too. Mud everywhere and cows rotting in the fields. My daughters looked pale, puffy; I fear their drinking water is tainted. They slept the whole night pressed up against me, their cold, moist little bodies still as corpses.

I wanted to bring them back with me, but with the Americans here now we can't risk Doña Morales finding out. The husband is a big shot at the company where Doña Morales's husband used to work—she'd take his word over ours. Luis had the opposite thought, he can help his family more in D.F., making money with the car—he basically runs a taxi service in the summertime when our boss is away. Doña Morales doesn't know that, or maybe she does, because despite how poorly she pays us she's always grumbling that Luis and I take advantage of her, an old widow. But this—keeping us in D.F. when she has fled and the city is sinking back into the lake it came out of, just to make a few American dollars—this is her revenge.

We've been here for a week now and it has rained all day every day. Dan has a car– a black Landrover, to be precise—that picks him up in the morning and whisks him away, but I've been stuck in the house all week with Ash, who refuses to eat anything solid, and has gone back to nursing full time. I did manage one trip to the market at the beginning of the week with Luis and the baby to stock up on essentials. I fumbled my way through the aisles snatching up whatever products looked familiar, not wanting to keep Luis waiting. It was a big, newish market (this is a fancy part of town), but poorly stocked. Whole aisles were bare and a lot of the packaging was water stained. *Mucha lluvia*, I said to Luis in the car on the way home, and he pursed his lips and sighed. When we got back to the house, he wouldn't let me replace the food we'd eaten or even take money for it— perhaps it was some horrible breach of etiquette, what we did, or perhaps he was just in a hurry. He took off as soon as we'd unloaded the groceries, he's always going somewhere in that car.

No, that's not right; I did get out one other time this week. During a rare pause in the rain, I sprinted to the Casa Azul with Ash in the stroller. The electric blue walls of the house glowed through the mist as I rounded the corner and raced up to the doors, Ash giggling the whole time as if it were all a game, instead of what it was, his desperate mother endangering his safety so she could say at the very least that she'd been to Kahlo's house! But Kahlo's house was closed, though it was meant to be open, and a single raindrop splashing onto Ash's chubby knee was enough to send us racing back home over the broken sidewalks.

Dan made some inquiries at the office and it seems the museum has been closed for repairs for some time now, but the director is willing to open it up and show me around. "Get Dolores to watch Ash," Dan said, as if it's that easy, but I may as well try.

The American has rushed off to an appointment somewhere. I, too, like to take advantage of these moments without rain, to run to the laundry room, to sweep the mud from the patio and the water pooled by the doors out into the courtyard, but her little son isn't happy that she's left him behind. He cries and cries; he won't stop till we go back to my room. It's just the right size for him; he walks around grabbing whatever catches his eye. This is our little game, he grabs at something, I put it up higher, he grabs at something else.

The phone rings in the kitchen, I run to get it. I bring it back into my room and give the baby a set of plastic containers to play with as I talk. He sits down with a thump on his diapered behind; I have a hurried conversation with my daughters. The rain has stopped for a brief moment there, too; they've run to the corner market to call me. "Come home, Mama," they breathe into the phone. "Grandma's sick, she can't get out of bed." I tell them to put the shopkeeper on the line, she knows my sister and will get a message to her. The little boy has started to fuss and cry; I tell my children not to worry and hang up.

I try giving the baby a strawberry Yakult but he won't take it. I tickle him under his arms and he laughs, but I can't help feeling there's something wrong with him. His eyes bulge, and his skin is pale and slimy. He reminds me of an axolotl, the walking fish that lives in the mud at the bottom of Lake Xochimilco. What's happening to our children?

Kahlo's house impressed me more than I thought it would: the tiled studio with its bold display of easel, wheelchair, corset; the deep red and purple skirts with which she surrounded her pain; the death mask wrapped in a grey rebozo; the defiant sunniness of her yellow kitchen. A stage set for the performance of Kahlo, but the performance of Kahlo, when understood as her life and not something just for the cameras, is actually quite moving. And to think all I knew before this was Kahlo of the feminist eyebrows!

The museum director was stooped, severe, dressed all in black with a beakish nose and steel grey hair. She's the interim director, she told me, but I don't know the things she's between—interim the expansion of the museum, interim its closure? Whole sections of the house were closed off with plastic sheeting and I could hear the sound of water dripping, but there weren't any work crews in sight. She took me through the open rooms but said very little, watching me indifferently, almost scornfully. She came to life only twice, once in front of the unfinished portrait of Stalin on Frida's easel in the studio, and again while looking at *Henry Ford Hospital.*

"*That* was their mistake!" she hissed, pointing at Stalin. Startled by her force of expression, I stepped back from the easel. "You probably don't know who this is, given the American educational system, but that's where Frida and Diego went wrong. To cast off Trotsky for Stalin, a great thinker for a thug! To scrap the dream of worldwide revolution for socialism in one country! And now look where we are—on the verge of collapse."

I wasn't sure whether she meant "we" as in Mexico, or "we" as in the world, but I nodded. Maybe Trotsky would've been better than Stalin; I wasn't educated well enough to know. "Of course, first Frida took him into her bed," she muttered scornfully. "That's all she could think of to do with Trotsky. To get back at that big baby, Diego, and feel a part of things."

It wasn't exactly the speech I'd been expecting to hear from the director of the Frida Kahlo museum. I was still in the throes of my first encounter with that lovely place, and it seemed to me unfair. So they didn't end capitalism, I wanted to say, didn't it matter that they lived their lives fully, that they followed their passions—didn't it matter that they tried? But she was clearly not the kind of person who gives points for living and trying.

She let loose again in the last room, in front of *Henry Ford Hospital.* "Everyone says, look at the pain in this picture, how brave Frida was to paint her miscarriage, the end of all her hopes and dreams to have a little Diegito! A little Diegito!" She nearly spat. "She didn't want that pregnancy. She was afraid it would kill her. He was already suffocating her, the great artist."

"And what about Frida's own practice?" I ventured timidly. "A child might've taken her away from her work."

She shrugged. "Art is not the most important thing in the world."

"But art gives us hope," I persisted weakly. "As long as we can create something new, there's still hope."

The director peered at me curiously. "Are you an artist?"

"A writer," I croaked. "I mean, I want to write."

"And you have a child?"

I nodded. "A little boy."

She smiled triumphantly. "So then you know, art is not the most important thing in the world."

A group of tourists milling around the front door caught sight of us through the second floor window and began pointing and shouting. A tall Northern European in a clear poncho stood out on the pavement and stared up fiercely at the director. "Please!" he yelled finally, pink with anger.

But she turned away from the window without so much as a nod—again, very strange, considering her position. I looked at a few more paintings and then she led me downstairs and across the muddy courtyard, cracking open one of the big wooden doors to let me out and slamming it shut after me. I hurried past the tourists, who caught at my sleeves, questioning me in their perfect English. "How did you get in?" "Why were you given a tour?" "How much did you pay her?" "When will the museum re-open to the public?" I was filled with a terrible sense of foreboding, and futility. I don't know what came over me—her mood was contagious. "Go home!" I hissed, breaking free of their grasp. "Go home!"

I've spoken with the girls again. Things back home have gone from bad to worse. My mother has come down with typhoid, and they're no longer going to school. The school building has flooded, and in my mother's house, too, there's standing water. Here, Luis is gone from morning till night, ferrying people out of the city. They pay him in diapers, mangos, clothing; he's filled the laundry room with goods.

The front courtyard is under water now but Luis has laid down a crude boardwalk so the Americans can get in and out. We've tried calling Dona Morales in Los Angeles, but she doesn't answer. Someone should tell the Americans this isn't normal, someone should tell them to leave—someone they will listen to. You can't even walk across the plaza any more, Luis tells me, it's a lake. The fountain with the two bronze coyote statues is barely visible, only the tips of their ears and muzzles poke out of the water.

But still, the husband works nonstop, while the woman rattles around the house with her little axolotl son. The other day she came in as I was trying to repair the leaky skylight in the master bathroom with trash bags and tape.

"No! The light!" she cried in her child's Spanish. She pointed at the rain falling gently into the tub and then at the drain and shrugged her shoulders, as if to say, a little rain in a bathtub is no big deal.

I peeled the trash bag off—it's not my house that's falling down around her ears—and she smiled as if we'd come to some big understanding. Then she asked where I was from, and when I said Veracruz, she rushed into the bedroom and came back with a guidebook, her finger on a photograph of the Dance of the Flyers, the pole dance men do in Papantla, circling their ropes to the ground. "My village," I said to her, placing my hand on my heart.

She nodded eagerly. "I want to go there."

"Of course! We'll take you," I lied.

"Yes, yes!" she cried. She's dying to go somewhere, anywhere. I heard Luis stifle a laugh out on the landing, and felt a little ashamed. But no one performs the Dance of the Flyers anymore anyway. It's a dance for rain.

Dan says he's making headway, but he's nowhere near done. He thinks I'm overreacting to the weather. "I know it sucks being stuck inside all day," he says, "but why not use the time to write? Arrange with Dolores for a nice big chunk of time every day."

"I don't think Dolores has nice big chunks of time every day," I say. "She's running around putting pots under leaks and taping up skylights."

"It's like that everywhere," he says, shaking his head. "This is the worst rainy season anyone can remember, and that's saying something for Mexico City. You should see the office."

"And that woman, the Kahlo Museum director," I say, whisking Ash away from a puddle that's mysteriously appeared under the coffee table in the TV room, where we sit in front of a snowy set, unable to get a picture. "To listen to her, you'd think it was the end of the world."

Dan stretches and yawns. "Well, she took a nice little sum off the company to show you around, so it can't be ending quite yet."

"Do you think we'll know when the world is ending?" I ask, resting my chin on Ash's bald head. Isn't he old enough to have hair? "Or do you think we'll go on calling it climate change till the last syllable of recorded time?"

"The world isn't going to end. It's just going to become less habitable."

"That's comforting."

"We'll be fine. Don't worry about Ash."

"I wasn't worrying about Ash. I was worrying about the *world*."

Dan smiles and squeezes my shoulder. My rants give him a chance to put his marriage philosophy into practice. He's convinced that if we're always kind and generous with one another, our marriage will outlast everyone else's. I think he got the idea from a post on Facebook—he mentioned it to me at the time—but he's since taken it on as his own personal truth. If we're kind and generous with each other, our marriage will survive the fact that we have less and less in common, that he has gone to work for the company, that I have gone to work for the baby, that the time when we were college kids together, spending our days in the same classes—short story workshops, gender studies seminars—our nights in the same twin bed, is so far in the past it's as if those were different people.

It's important to him, though, that I keep writing, that my dream stay the same, because then it's not as obvious that his has changed. Dan's good at his job, he likes being good at his job, he dreams of being even better at it—why should I begrudge him that? He keeps me on an even keel, he tells me I'm a great mom, if I ever write a story again, he'll be the first to read it. He was excited to learn the office was located in Coyoacan, someone told him it was the most bohemian neighborhood in Mexico City. He thought it would inspire me, to walk the cobbled streets of Coyoacan.

Last night I dreamed Luis and I were in a little rowboat, paddling toward Veracruz. Getting home had become so easy now that the water was above the rooftops, and we laughed and sang, making our way through all of the other little boats heading home too. Out in the countryside, we came to my daughters, floating on their backs in the water. They were wearing their white communion dresses, and their long black hair fanned out from their heads like snakes. "Hi, Mama," they said, and they too seemed at peace. I knew they had drowned, but this no longer seemed so hard. They kept pace with the boat and we traveled as a family; I felt happier and more content than I have in a long time, paddling alongside my dead daughters. When I woke up, I was seized with horror. That's how I started my day.

They're saying a storm will come through D.F. this weekend that will make all the other storms look weak in comparison; they're saying it will flood the city from corner to corner, that the neighborhoods will once more resemble the Aztec chinampas, the floating gardens that were here at the very beginning. But we're not sticking around to see; we're heading for Veracruz as soon as Luis has secured the fuel we need.

The city's emptying out fast—millions of people have already disappeared. They're getting away from the dirty cops, who're even dirtier now that the narco-traffickers have packed up and gone. They're going to where they can see trouble coming from a distance, to where they can grow food—and if they can't grow food, to where they know someone who can, someone who cares if their children live or die.

This morning we were in the courtyard loading things into the car (Luis wants to bring all of it—we've got bags of stuff strapped to the roof) when the American came out with her baby. "Okay to leave?" she asked, holding him out to me. I took him in my arms, but shook my head. "We're going to Veracruz tomorrow. I have too much to do."

"Veracruz!" she said. "What for?"

I hesitated, wanting to tell her the truth, wanting to tell her they should leave too. But Luis wouldn't risk it, he's afraid we'll lose the car, that they'll tell Doña Morales and she'll send somebody for it before we can manage to get out of here. "A fiesta!" he nearly shouted at her, nodding and smiling. "Next time, you'll come too!"

She took the baby back and walked sadly inside. I don't know what will happen to the Americans. Luis says not to worry; the company will look after them. "But even if it doesn't," he says, "don't worry about the Americans. The Americans have never worried about you."

When the rain finally let up this afternoon, I had to get out of the house. I tried leaving the baby with Dolores, but she didn't have time—Luis says they're going to a fiesta in Veracruz tomorrow, though they didn't look like people going to a fiesta. They looked harried and stressed out and they're packing that little car way too full, it's never going to make it over the mountains. I wonder if Mrs. Morales just lets them come and go like this?

My plan was to visit Trotsky's house, which my guidebook said would be open. I didn't actually expect it to be open, but it gave me a destination, a goal, a reason to brave the rain. It was twenty blocks from the house over rough and broken sidewalks and around knee-deep puddles, with an hour spent waiting out a squall inside an eerily empty shoe emporium. Ash no longer agitates to get out of his stroller in situations like that; he sits quietly the whole time, watching the rain. It thumped against the storefront, rattling the glass, and he couldn't tear his eyes away.

I worry about Ash in this place. He's so pale from being inside all the time, his eyes have big circles under them, and the few hairs that have grown in are somehow always wet, stuck to the sides of his head. Last night I dreamed I was crossing over the landing to nurse him, to lie with him as I do most nights on the TV room couch, listening to the thunder crashing in the distance or the rain pounding on the roof. But in the dream when I got to his travel crib, there was no baby there, only a large white salamander-like creature, with bulging eyes and clammy skin. I picked it up and looked into its golden eyes, understanding that it was Ash and feeling neither horror nor grief at the realization but instead an enormous relief. This creature, I knew, could survive this world.

When the rain stopped, we exited the shoe emporium and continued on to Trotsky's house. The sun was out for the first time since we arrived in Mexico City. Ash turned his little face towards it like a dying plant and I felt my mood lift. Perhaps tomorrow there would be more sun and then more the day after that and then it would just be sunny, and the endless rain would be something we talked about as a freak weather event, not our nemesis, our captor.

The little yellow house appeared surprisingly cheerful as we approached. It was hard to imagine that this could be where Trotsky was assassinated after leaving the Casa Azul, until you looked more closely and spotted the stone gun tower cobbled onto the flat roof and the bricked-in windows facing the street. Then the house appeared abject and mutilated, an architectural calamity of the brutal twentieth century. I was struck by the amateurish quality of the fortifications— it was almost as if Trotsky hadn't truly believed he could be killed, even after the first assassination attempt, or, more likely, hadn't truly believed he could survive.

To my surprise, the doors to the courtyard were open and people were hurrying in and out. I wheeled Ash over to the entrance and a young man stopped to help me lift the stroller over the threshold. "What's happening?" I asked him once we were safely inside, gesturing to the people bringing in suitcases and boxes and sandbags from their cars. He paused before answering, in English, "On the weekend, there will be a very big storm. We will sleep here."

"To protect the museum?" I asked, still not understanding. "To save Trotsky's house?"

He laughed and lit a cigarette, waving the smoke away from Ash. "Trotsky, that asshole? No, the walls are very thick here, do you see? Three feet in some places, to keep out the bullets. We hope they will also keep out the wind and the water."

"Have the authorities given you permission to be here?"

"Authorities?" he grinned.

With that, he disappeared into one of the buildings, and Ash began to wail. A cloud had passed in front of the sun, which was our cue to leave. We raced home, but we didn't beat the rain. We were two blocks from the house when it started, and soaked to our underwear by the time we made it inside.

That night, Dan revealed his first doubts. It wasn't my story about Trotsky's house that disturbed him. "Sounds to me like a bunch of anarchists trying to justify a squat," was his response to that. No, it was the fact that his office manager hadn't shown up to work.

"We've been missing people, a couple each day maybe. But, you know, clerical workers. This guy's crucial. Not sure how I'm going to do it without him."

"Can't you just quit? What if they're right? What if we're in for a terrible storm this weekend?"

Dan grew serious and I felt a matrimonial lecture coming on. "Hey, this is one of those moments when I really need your support," he said, holding my gaze. "I'm still proving myself at the company and they need to know I can close the branch down and take care of our customers with minimum disruption."

"Do they have any idea how bad it is down here?"

"They don't want to know. They just want me to get the job done."

"But it doesn't *matter*, Dan. All you're doing is saving them a little bit of money!"

My husband looked at me for a long moment, giving me time to move back in the direction of kindness and generosity, but I sat in stony silence, eyes averted.

"I have to be up early," he muttered finally, and left the room, which somehow felt like a tiny victory.

This morning was sunny, a more beautiful day than I can ever remember, and I've lived ten years in D.F. So sunny and beautiful, I asked Luis if he thought we really had to go. Maybe we were fools to rush off. Maybe the rains were over now and the city would soon dry out, maybe the restaurants would re-open, and the sidewalk cafes, and the balloon men would once more wander the plaza with toys for the children and for the lovers pretending to be children. The Americans would leave and Doña Morales would come back to plague us with her bad moods and incessant demands and we could go on as we were before.

"You can believe that if you want," he said, shaking his head. "I'm still going."

But of course, even if I believed that, I had to go, because who knew how things were in Veracruz? My sister wasn't answering her cell phone, and the phone at the corner store rang and rang.

The American stopped me in the passageway. "You're going now?" she asked. "To Veracruz?"

"Yes," I said, brushing by.

"Please." She caught my sleeve. "They say there's going to be a big storm. Is it true?"

I looked over my shoulder at Luis and saw his head was buried in the trunk. "Yes, Friday," I whispered. "You should go. You should go."

She nodded slowly. I thought she understood. Then she looked out into the courtyard and I knew she understood. "I don't think Mrs. Morales would want—" she started to say, pointing at the car, but Luis was opening up the courtyard doors with one hand and waving me into the car with the other, and I didn't stay to hear her finish.

It was sunny again on Wednesday and Thursday morning, but the storm arrived earlier than Dolores said it would—in the middle of the afternoon on Thursday. At first it just seemed like a particularly bad rain, not something in a whole other category. Dan went off to work as usual in the morning and Ash and I spent most of the day watching the water rise in the courtyard. I stuffed towels in among the sandbags and occupied myself and the baby with wringing them out. It wasn't really that different from other days, except for the need for more active home maintenance, and the fact that Dan actually came home at dinnertime.

"What's to eat?" he asked absently, as I struggled to open the door and let him in.

"Quesadilla and yogurt," I said. "Or that's what Ash is having, theoretically. What are you doing here? You're never home this early."

"Job's over."

"You mean you're finished?" I asked excitedly, following him into the kitchen, where Ash sat in his highchair.

"No, I mean nobody came into work today, except for me and my driver. I called Martin in New York, and he couldn't believe we were still down here. I guess this is supposed to be the mother of all storms."

I didn't say I told you so. That one time, I was kind and generous.

"He says I should've talked more with the locals, gotten a better read on the situation," Dan said, sinking into a chair. "I've been too focused on the job. He made some good points, things to keep in mind for next time."

I stared at him. "What do you mean, next time?"

He shrugged. "Anyway, they're getting us out tomorrow morning. We're going to LA."

"How?"

"They've got a guy."

"A guy?"

"You know, one of those guys that does extractions. Probably a former Navy Seal or a Marine or something."

"Really? One of those guys?"

He nodded. "We better start packing. He's coming at 6 am."

I got up, but to my surprise he didn't move. "What is it?" I asked.

"It's pretty bad out there," he said, staring at Ash without seeing him. "The avenues are still passable but the side streets are completely underwater. I looked up one and saw all these dogs—all different shapes and sizes—paddling round and round, trying to find a place to land. My driver said people have been letting them out as they leave the city."

"No people stranded out there, though, right? Just dogs?"

"Dog!" Ash echoed, and Dan smiled at him distractedly, avoiding my question.

"Hey," I said, unnerved by his silence. "What if the company guy doesn't come?"

"What? Oh." He stretched and yawned, back to his old self again. "The company guy always comes. That's why we're with the company."

Around four that morning, while I was nursing the baby in the TV room, there was a loud crash. Ash pulled off the breast, eyes round, and I rushed to the door with him on my hip. I could see Dan standing in our bedroom doorway on the other side of the atrium, but there was a waterfall between us, pent up rainwater spilling off the roof in a giant slab, down through the shattered skylight and onto the floor below.

"Kitty!" Ash squealed as a drowned cat went by.

The flow tapered off once all of the water pooled on the roof had made its way down into the living room, and then it was just the rain coming softly through the jagged hole in the glass. Ash watched it peacefully and so did I, as Dan sloshed around down below, moving our bags to higher ground. It was a relief, letting the rain in at last.

And then the company guy came and we got out of the city. He wasn't a Navy Seal or a Marine, he was Miguel, the same man who'd been driving Dan back and forth to work every day, in the same black Landrover, just maybe they paid him a little more, or maybe not, I don't know. Oh, and Dan said he'd put on bigger tires. The thirty-hour drive to L.A. was hellish in every way you'd imagine, with the fateful symmetry of a fairytale—three times the car stalled and we had to get out and push, three times we drove past scenes of horror and destitution without stopping, three times I told Dan I was leaving him.

And then we were standing in the drop-off zone of a luxury hotel in downtown LA and I was trying to get him to give Miguel the rest of our cash. "He saved our lives, just give it to him!" I yelled and finally he did, begrudgingly, because he was convinced the company had already paid him handsomely. Miguel got back into the jacked-up Landrover and drove away, and I followed him with tears streaming down my cheeks— only a few steps, but far enough I guess that Dan felt he had to come after me. Placing a hand on either shoulder, he wheeled me around gently to face the lobby entrance, where Ash sat in his muddy stroller, squirming in the sun.

Who Will Sit With Maman?

The window units are leaking. The tenants call and call, but there's only me to attend to them. My brother comes now and then, to sit with Maman, but he can't be bothered with the building. He's off doing clever things with money. When he gets enough, when he's established, he tells Maman, he's going to send some opportunities our way. "Opportunities?" Maman echoes.

My brother has an air-conditioned feel to him when he breezes in (they all do, the ones who live in the New City). His hands are cool against Maman's brow, and she groans with pleasure at his touch. But after a few minutes, he starts to sweat, loosens his tie, rolls up his sleeves. He asks for a glass of water and drinks it in one long draught, his Adam's apple bobbing up and down on his smooth-shaven neck. Finally, he has to leave. His world is so different from ours now, he can't stay. Maman gazes at him with filmy eyes, trying to hold him, but she's really looking past his shoulder at the open door. Wherever she senses light, she thinks it's my brother. But it was always that way, even when she could see.

He has a wife in one of the New City towers. They married on a Tahitian island that was once owned by a famous movie star, in an eco-hotel with a cooling system designed by the star himself—one of those exceptional individuals to whom my brother is always drawing our attention. The movie star's cooling system draws water from the

sea and desalinates it. That's the way to go, my brother says. That's
the way they have gone in the New City. But we're too far from the
sea to go that way.

We didn't attend the wedding. My brother invited us, of course, he
even said he would buy our tickets—it was a pretty scene he staged
in Maman's sickroom that day, smoothing the wrinkled skin of her
hand with his thumb. But Maman said she felt too weak to travel, she
would only ruin his good time.

"I'll go to Tahiti," I said loudly over her sighing, if only to put an
end to his little play. "I'll come to your wedding." My brother's face
hardened quickly with resentment and fear, fear that I would be the
one to ruin his good time, then softened when he found his answer.
"But . . . Maman," he said, raising her hand to his lips adoringly. "Who
will sit with Maman?"

We've never met his wife. I don't even know if they're still married,
or if he already has another one. I never saw the wedding pictures—he
showed them to Maman on his phone. Of course she couldn't make
them out, but she marveled over the light in the palm of his hand.

2B must be attended to first. The tenant has asthma, he cannot breathe.
The window unit is spitting puffs of smoke into his room—smoke
or dust, he can't determine which. But when he switches off the unit,
the heat is like an oven and he can't breathe then either.

I climb the stairs to 2B with my canvas bag of tools. It's surely the
most valuable thing in the building and I keep a close watch on it at all
times. If this bag were to disappear, I would never be able to replace
its contents. It's all anyone wants now, all anyone needs—at least
in our part of town, which is crumbling day by day into the desert,
seared by the hot winds. The ocean breezes have all been rerouted to
the New City, or so my brother tells us. It was a gaming tycoon who
figured out how to do it—another one of those Renaissance men he
models himself after.

I can hear the tenant coughing and wheezing before I get to his
door—he wasn't exaggerating his need. The door's ajar. I knock once

and push it open.

He's irritable, 2B, irritable and angry. He startles when I enter, then swivels his chair toward the window without a word. When I walk over to the unit, I can see him glaring at the little puffs of dust it continues to produce in place of cool air. I turn it off and open my tool bag.

All of the tenants have studio apartments, one large room in which their lives are fully on display, which makes for an uneasy intimacy when I'm on my rounds. I've been working for ten minutes, cleaning the caked red dust from the filters and vents, before 2B even speaks.

"It's an oven in here!" he gasps, pulling at the neck of his sweat-soaked t-shirt. We're both sweating profusely. It's not that the air has gotten any hotter—it's simply more still. It sits on us, a dead weight.

"Do you have an inhaler?" I ask.

2B laughs at the idea, and the laugh turns into a terrible coughing fit that goes on and on, punctuated by great gasps. I don't stop to assist him, nor to find him assistance. We've been through this before. He just wants the window unit fixed.

I replace the filters and the vent panel and turn it on. Air comes out: it's not red, it's not dusty. It is a little cool. This is what we call fixing the unit.

I don't wait for the room to cool down. I don't wait for him to breathe. I have other units to repair.

The biggest unit is in Maman's bedroom. My brother found it in a dumpster in the New City—a hulking anachronism still in its box. But here it can only run when there's electricity to run it, a few hours here and there, so her room is only slightly cooler than the others. And she's no less irritable and angry than the tenants, because she's dying and her favorite son lives in the New City with a wife she's never met.

"Where have you been?" she demands when I enter her room.

"Fixing the unit in 2B," I say, heaving onto the armchair by her bed.

"Why do you bother?" she spits, dragging herself higher onto her pillows. "None of them pays any rent."

"He has asthma," I say.

"He is fat," she replies.

Maman was not always like this. It was my brother who turned her against the tenants. When she was well, she was their mother, too. "Maman!" they cried to her from their sickbeds, their childbeds, their deathbeds even, and Maman was there.

"Turn him out," she wheezes. "Turn them all out!"

"Where are they supposed to go?" I say. I, too, am irritable and angry. "Do you want the gendarmes to get them?"

The police are charged with keeping us away from the New City. They stop anyone out on the street now after dark, and men from the former colonies, which is most of the men in our quarter, are taken down to the station or—depending on the mood of the gendarmes— beaten and left in the gutter.

"You're too soft," she says, lying back down again. "You've always been too soft. You cried when you were a boy—your brother, never. He would stand up to them."

Neither of them knows I've told the tenants they don't have to pay me. They have no jobs, they have no money. Like me, like her, like everyone living in the shadow of the New City, they're simply waiting to see what happens next. There are forces at work, and they originate elsewhere. The few that do pay are drawing on their savings, and when their savings run out, I'll let them stay for free too. They're not defying me. We have an understanding.

4C is a bright-eyed old man who drinks tea all day long. "It's good to drink hot tea in hot weather," he says. "We do this in India. It cools the body down." He has a bird named Plato, a gray parrot who eats out of his hand and whom he has taught to say, "Be kind, for everyone you meet is fighting a harder battle." The parrot's voice is droll, his impersonation of the philosopher makes us laugh. "But it's true, you know," the old man says, when we've stopped laughing.

Today I bring him a repaired window unit. I lug it up the stairs and careen into his room, landing it on the sill with a crash (I'm not an especially muscular man). The repair shops are all closed, so I've started trying to fix the compressors myself, a process of trial and error. I replace his unit, plug it in, and turn it on.

"Sit, sit!" he urges me. He has made a fresh pot of tea. I sit and wait with him for the room to cool.

"I feel it!" he says after a few minutes, straining forward in his chair. "It's working!"

"No," I say. "It's no cooler than before."

"Yes, yes, I tell you!" he says. "It is better! Thank you."

"I'll take it back down," I say. "I'll try again."

"No need," he says graciously, with a wave of his hand. "You fixed it."

The old man's make-believe grows tiresome. My battle's no harder than his—he's burning alive. We're all burning alive. I down my tea and leave the broken air conditioner rattling away in his apartment.

The heat is very bad today. When the heat is very bad, Maman makes me call my brother.

"She's suffering today," I tell him. "The heat."

"I can't get away," he says. "Tell her I'll come tomorrow."

"Tomorrow?" she asks when I get off the phone, in a small voice muffled by pillows.

"Yes, tomorrow."

And that's usually enough, though he won't come tomorrow. Enough to get her to sit up and drink some water, eat her yogurt. Plain yogurt is all she takes now; I buy it at the farmer's market outside the New City wall. A quart of yogurt can be had for the price of an antique armoire, a headboard, a good length of copper piping. I'm slowly stripping 3A and 4C for this purpose. They've been empty for months.

3B doesn't seem to care about her window unit, but she calls on me frequently for other, smaller repairs. In her apartment, she stays cool by wearing only a bra and panties. I enjoy making her other, smaller repairs.

Today she greets me sitting at the kitchen table, and holds out a flyer. She's having a party and she wants me to come. She's said this before, but I've never heard party noises on the appointed day. If I'd heard party noises, I might have stopped in out of curiosity. To see who was there, what people did nowadays at a party.

But today she's very insistent. Her flyer has a crude unicorn drawing on it, and the words "White Party" scribbled above.

"What is a White Party?" I ask.

"It has a theme," she says, leaning forward excitedly. "Everyone must wear white."

"Ah," I say. "Why?"

My questions deflate her. She shrugs and rests her face in her hands. "It's the theme," she says hollowly.

"I'll be there," I say quickly, looking over the flyer. There's no date. "When is it?"

"Tonight."

"Tonight!"

"Yeah," she says, taking her hands away from her face. "You got plans?"

I blush and look at the floor. Tonight's plan is the same as last night's and the night before. After I finish my last repair, I'll go back downstairs to sit with Maman until we both fall asleep.

3B rubs her eyes. "Sorry," she mutters.

I pick up my tool bag and head over to the sleeping area. I'm there to fix a wobbly shelf. It's not really so wobbly—all it takes is two or three turns of the screws.

My last call of the day is 4B. The tenant is a slender, brilliant young man, a classical violinist. He practices night and day, pushing himself relentlessly, as if preparing for an important concert. No one complains. The music provides an elevating soundtrack to our lives.

But now it's almost too hot to play. That's why 4B has called me.

He may have to stop if I can't fix the unit. Nobody wants that.

He's rail thin when he answers the door—he's sweated away whatever meat he had on his bones when I last saw him. He smiles wanly, his hand fluttering towards the air conditioner.

Unfortunately, it's the compressor.

"I'll have to take it out," I say. "I need to take it down to my workroom."

4B looks stricken. "Okay," he says softly.

As I'm prying the unit from the window, I tell him about the party in 3B. "A White Party," he echoes. "But I'm not white."

"It's not like that," I explain. "She means you must wear white."

"Ah," he says. "Why?"

"It's the theme," I say. "She wants it to have a theme."

He nods, mulling it over.

"Bring your violin," I grunt, swinging the unit out of the window and hurtling towards the door. "We'd love to hear you play."

4B nods again, unconvinced.

I don't expect to see the old man from 4C at the party, but he's there, drinking calvados. Calvados! Where did it come from?

"My last bottle," he says modestly. "Can you see how dusty it is? It had fallen behind the liquor cabinet."

He pours me a thimble's worth. "The bottle was only half-full," he says apologetically. I see the others have thimble-worths too, and are nursing them quietly around the table. Except for our hostess— she's made a punch out of mouthwash and is drinking a mug of it while dancing alone in the corner. Mouthwash! Where did it come from?

2B sits by the window, looking up at the moon. He has a thimble's worth of calvados *and* a cup of punch. It's hot, but not as hot as the day. He breathes easier now, his massive chest rising and falling in a bright white guayabera.

The violinist steals into the room and looks around, then hides his instrument in the corner. I nod to him and smile, but he looks away, embarrassed. Our hostess takes him by the hand, but he doesn't wish to dance.

He's dressed in white like the rest of us, but whereas I have on a white t-shirt and painter's pants, he's wearing white slacks, a white tuxedo shirt and white patent leather shoes. The only one who can match him is our hostess, in her Mexican wedding dress, a fake camellia in her hair.

I wish he would dance with her. I'd like to see them dance together. I'm just about to ask them to when the power goes out and the music stops. She shrieks and curses, kicks the stereo. He draws her gently by both elbows into the sleeping area. Perhaps they will dance after all.

The rest of us sit in silence, licking our empty Calvados glasses. We can't quite make up our minds to go. The moonlight streams in at the window, picking up the white of our garments. We're like the lost crew of a ghost ship, frozen in time.

I fumble my way into the corner and unearth the violin. I press it into his hands, along with the bow. Our hostess sits on the edge of her bed picking at the quilt. He raises the violin to his chin and begins to play.

Like I said, we've all heard his music before, we hear it every day, but never before in the same room. We put down our glasses. She looks up from her quilt. May we stay in this moonlit darkness forever, listening to the racing notes and watching him feel his way towards freedom.

The next day my brother brings a group of investors to see the building. The tenants and I are wrecked and defenseless; we drank the mouthwash punch when the power came back on and danced until it went off again just before dawn. Our doors are unlocked, our white garments strewn about, we lie sprawled in compromising positions, though our breath smells surprisingly good. The investors step purposefully through the mess, they only have eyes for the building: the high ceilings, the built-ins and wood floors, the good, clean lines. Maman has gussied herself up to meet them, but they pass by her door without entering—only my brother ducks in to talk to her in a low voice before quickly rejoining the group. For me, he has sharper words. "This is my brother, the current building manager," he says scornfully. "You can see what he's done with the property! You stripped the upstairs apartments, didn't you, you degenerate!"

The investors stand impassively—all except one, a slim blonde with a blinding white smile. His new wife, perhaps? "How marvelous!" she cries, pointing at me.

I sit up, clutching my head, trying to understand in what way I am marvelous. But her finger doesn't move. She's pointing at the bay window.

"Are there more of those?" she asks my brother.

"In my mother's bedroom," he answers, waving them into the hallway. Now Maman will finally get to meet her.

Afterwards, I learn that they walked into 3B's apartment and found her making love to the violinist. "Back in five minutes!" my brother said brusquely, stepping out and shutting the door. 3B threw her shoe at the door, then opened it and threw her other shoe at the back of my brother's head. Magnificent woman.

Some time later, I walk into Maman's bedroom to find her and my brother wreathed in smiles. He has an open bottle of champagne in his hand—she's even drinking a little.

"The building is sold!" they tell me in unison.

"Sold!" I gasp.

"Yes!" Maman croaks. "Isn't it wonderful?"

"It's not a huge some of money," my brother says, "but it will provide Maman with a nice tidy income."

"But how?" I ask, still dumbstruck. I never thought it would actually happen. "Why would anyone from the New City want to live out here?"

My brother gazes at me coldly, though as usual he is sweating from every pore. "Do you ever turn on that tablet I gave you? When was the last time you read the news? The New City is expanding. It's right around the corner."

"They've renamed this the Historic Quarter," Maman says. "Our building will go on a registry. Everyone will want to live here."

"But Maman," I say. "It won't be our building."

My brother waves his hand. "Maman will be allowed to stay."

"And me?" I ask. "And the tenants?"

My brother smirks. "The tenants must go, of course. And you, well—you can't really expect them to keep you on?"

"You act as if you aren't one of the investors," I sneer. He's not going to win this one so easily. "The main investor, I'll wager. And your wife—did you even tell Maman that was your wife, the blonde who loves bay windows?"

This is a low blow—a lunge in the dark, really—but I can see by the way his face hardens that it has landed. Maman turns to him with a fish-eyed stare. "Your wife?" she whispers feebly, her hand fluttering to her heart.

My brother sets the champagne bottle down on her bedside table. "Get out," he says to me through clenched teeth.

"But . . . Maman?" I simper. "Who will sit with Maman?"

"You will not ruin this!" he howls.

She rolls over with her back to us. "Maman?" he says, gently touching her back. She doesn't answer. She doesn't move. Her nightgown sticks to her shoulder blades, which jut out sharply, like broken wings.

"I'm leaving now, Maman," he says softly. "I'll be back tomorrow." Still no response. He turns to go and staggers a bit under the weight of what we both know. She's going to die now.

From Maman's bay window, you can see a patch of dirt that was once a prodigious garden. She used to leave baskets of sun-ripened tomatoes in the lobby for the tenants, bags of sweet lemons, cut flowers in jars, sunflowers and delphinium—do you remember how it used to be? Now the earth is hard and riddled with cracks—many small, some large, like desiccated veins. You can no longer till it, your shovel clangs with the effort—and anyway, what's the point? Our wheezing old window units exacerbate the problem, but we can't turn them off. This is the case everywhere but in the New City, which is doused in desalinated water, a bright green insult on the horizon we try never to look at.

Maman was gone before the close of escrow—she simply gave up trying to eat after that, and eventually, to breathe—but the tenants and I remain. We received our notices, but the eviction date came and went and no one showed up to turn us out. The tenants all came to her funeral—they mourned sincerely, they shook my brother's hand. Some of them were brought into this world by Maman, they told him, and they wanted to see her out. But that's not what slowed down the process, we all know that. It's something beyond even my brother's control. The New City is biding its time.

Other timelines appear: 2B has lung cancer, it turns out; 3B and the violinist are expecting a baby—we focus on those eventualities and not the other. We gather in the coolest rooms, we pamper 2B and 3B in whatever ways we can—by and large, the mood is good. In the heat of the day we sit together at a table in front of Maman's window unit, playing cards, joking and laughing—yes, why not laugh? The gendarmes are circling the building, but they haven't taken it yet.

Meet Koko

I'm really getting up there —forty-four today. Penny threw me another goddamn kiddie party this morning, took me for a walk around the compound. Same thing, year after year. Made a video of me unwrapping gifts, narrating my raptures and disappointments. Like I care about any of that shit. I'm telling you, forty-four years is a long time to be treated like a baby.

But it's my own fault too. I mean, I have language. I could do something with it instead of lying around the trailer all day, watching TV and eating Cheetos. I'm lazy, I'll admit it. I'm an underperformer. But can you imagine my life if they knew how many signs I actually have? What my vocabulary really is? I try keeping our interactions as limited as possible, and Penny still bugs me all the time. "Flowers" "Sad" "Fake"—she can string a twenty-minute conversation out of just those three words.

"Fake" is usually directed at Penny, but she's so clueless. "No, honey, those flowers aren't fake!" she says. "Koko sad," I sign. "Penny fake! Penny fake!" "No, honey!" she says, "Those flowers Penny brought you are real!" Of course, she could know what I'm really saying and just be bullshitting for the camera. I wouldn't put it past her.

Yes, there comes a time when you have to look at your life and ask yourself, can I do better than this? I think that time is forty-four. And I think the answer is yes. My own mother died when she was eleven.

All this extra time I've been given, and what have I done with it?

I'm going to start by setting the record straight. If you're reading this, you're on the Gorilla Foundation website, looking at videos of me posted by Penny. Because that's where I'm putting this when I'm done. This is my counter-narrative. Yes, I did just use that word.

Meet Koko

In this video, I sign that I'm Koko, and I'm a gorilla. I really meant to say "guerrilla," but Penny hasn't taught me the sign for that. I'm a guerrilla for gorillas, sabotaging her apes-are-our-cousins project with my bad attitude and lazy signing.

"Gorillas are an endangered species," it says on the screen, and then cuts to me signing "Sad." Sure, I'm sad about that, but I sign sad about a hundred times a day. I figure if I sign it enough, someone at the Foundation will finally catch on and say, "Hey, Koko seems kind of depressed." But then Penny would probably fire them.

"I'm good," I sign in the video, patting myself on the back. But there's no inflection in the subtitles. "*I'm* good," is how I meant it. You guys are a bunch of monkey turds.

Don't get me wrong, I fell for the cousin rap too, back in the day—meaning back in the seventies, though I always thought of it more as a sisterhood. You had the one pale-skinned young human female—Jane—camping out with the chimpanzees, you had Dian tracking gorillas in the mist, and then you had Penny, who borrowed me from the San Francisco Zoo to do her doctoral research at Stanford and never gave me back. The idea was to raise me around humans, on the theory that language learning was a process of acculturation. If I bonded with Penny, I'd be motivated to communicate in ways she could understand.

And like I said, I was into it at first. I learned my whole vocabulary, as far as they know, in those first few years—all one thousand signs. I was dying to talk, I loved sitting on Penny's lap, running my fingers through her long hair the color of buttercups. "Flower," I signed, over and over again. Sweet little gorilla. Sweet little Penny.

But as time went on, my human sister started to annoy me. I knew a lot of words by then—I'd been listening carefully to Penny, to Penny bicker with Ron, to Penny's advisor drone on about primates and our abilities, and to Reggie the groundskeeper, who had a mouth on him. But she wasn't teaching me any of those signs. "Drink" "Food" "More" for three months running—I was dying of boredom! Plus, she used to put a leash around my neck and pull on it to get me to concentrate on my lesson. Could you get any more annoying?

"Meet Koko," I signed to her. "Meet Koko." At least meet me halfway! Jane went out into the jungle and for two years she was the lowest chimpanzee on the totem pole—she put in her time. But Penny set up shop with me in a trailer on Stanford land in Woodside, California. She used to tell reporters she started this project because she wanted to know what I was thinking, but she didn't, not really. No human really wants to know what gorillas are thinking.

Koko Critiques Her Painting

Penny and I have very different taste in art, which is another point of conflict. In this video, I'm making an abstract painting while Penny watches. It's obviously dreck. I'm hard on myself as an artist, but that's because I have standards. "Toilet!" I say about my painting. "Bad! Toilet!" "Oh no, honey," she assures me, "It's very good!" Look at that palette, those clumsy brush strokes, and tell me it's very good.

Koko Plays with a Yellow Balloon

In this one, Penny gives me a yellow balloon and tells me to do something "imaginative" with it. I love the color; I gaze at it, drinking it in. It's like a little sun brightening up our dingy trailer. But no, it has an artificial quality to it. It's fake. How interesting, a fake sun. The way man copies nature and then seeks to replace it. I'm starting to comment on this when Peggy interrupts me. "Juggle it! Come on, play with it!" I stare at her uncomprehendingly. I mean, I understand what she's saying, I just can't believe this is my interlocutor, for as many as eight hours a day. Is the woman capable of a complex thought?

Apparently not. She takes the yellow balloon, that bright, perfect orb, and draws a face on it. Then she gives it back to me. I start drawing hairs on it, black hairs all over it, and Penny suddenly understands. "Gorilla hairs!" she cries. "You're making it into a gorilla!"

"You," I sign at Penny, and then I pop the balloon. You're destroying this gorilla.

Koko 'Types' While Ron Films

Ron and Penny giggle as I "type" on Penny's laptop. Ron films most of my videos, but in this one Penny is filming him filming me. She congratulates herself on this very sophisticated bit of framing. Ron just keeps on filming. He never says much. He's Penny's research collaborator and also her mate, so much of their communication is unspoken.

I type crazily, hammering at the keyboard. I pick up the laptop and bring it close to my face, then turn it upside down. Penny ultimately has to rescue her computer from me. I have sufficiently convinced them I only know how to "type," not how to type. That means they will never check on me in the middle of the night to see if I'm using Penny's laptop, never think to open up the document titled "Meet Koko" on her desktop.

All Ball

When I was around thirteen or fourteen, Penny gave me a kitten. I'd been asking for it for over a year, but she kept giving me stuffed cats instead. "Fake!" "Bad!" "Sad!" I signed to her over and over again, until she finally got the message.

I called my new kitty All Ball because I enjoyed the rhyme. Also, there was an absurdist quality to my Manx cat, with its missing tail and squeaky little voice that put me in mind of the Dadaist sound poet Hugo Ball. But according to Penny in this video, I named it All Ball because I thought it looked like a ball.

You're told that when All Ball was run over by a car, I learned one of life's hardest lessons. That in loving All Ball, I experienced loss for the first time. And yes, it was sad when All Ball died. But I was taken from my mother, assholes. I already knew plenty about loss. Her warm, hairy body—gone. I fell ill as an infant at the San Francisco Zoo and they kept me in the nursery for many months. When I got out, it was too late to bond with her and they didn't know what to do with me. So they gave me to Penny.

Plus the way they told me about All Ball—so fake! Ron was all set up to film my reaction. You see me signing "Bad" "Sad" "Bad" "Frown," but that's not about All Ball. It's about the fact that they put me on camera when they told me the news. "Later, privately, Koko expressed her grief," the voiceover says, and you see the outside of the trailer and hear me howling. I was indeed expressing my grief in that moment: that this was my life; that these were to be my companions for the rest of my days.

Koko Practices Motherhood With Doll

When Penny was in her late thirties, she became obsessed with the idea of my having a baby. "Koko wants to be a mother so much," she kept telling everybody. "She just wants a little baby to hold." She started calling around to zoos to see if she could find me a mate—first Michael, then Nduke. I'm not sure what she was expecting. I mean, they were good-looking guys, but very poor conversationalists. Would you mate with someone you couldn't talk to? Someone who threw poop and regurge at you to get your attention?

Penny and Ron were collaborators—that's the kind of relationship I was looking for. Though during that period, they argued a lot. "Do you want a baby or don't you want one?" Ron yelled. "Just tell me what you want!" "It's not that simple!" Penny sobbed. "I want one and I don't want one."

That's when she started giving me dolls to play with—gorilla and human. In this video, I press a human baby doll to my chest, but I'm not "practicing motherhood," as the title suggests. I'm just helping Penny work through some issues.

Koko Eats All Her Veggies

Here you see me eating cooked vegetables out of a Tupperware with a spoon. "You're really enjoying those, aren't you, honey?" Penny says. This would seem inconsequential were it not for the fact that a group of former employees recently sued the Gorilla Foundation, claiming that Penny and Ron had endangered my physical welfare by feeding me junk food and allowing me to lounge around the trailer all day and never exercise. Penny's worried the lawsuit is going to drain the Foundation's coffers and prevent our move to Hawaii, so this video is really about public relations. I honestly think some nice roughage— some giant cabbage leaves, for instance—would've made for better optics, but she always gets a kick out of seeing me eat with a spoon.

The plan is to move our operation out of Woodside and over to a seventy-acre gorilla preserve in Maui, where I'll supposedly be more open to mating with Ndume. Yes, that's right, Penny still thinks I'm going to have a baby.

Do Gorillas Feel Empathy?

In this video, Penny interprets my reaction to a shitty movie she makes me watch with her all the time: *Tea with Mussolini*. I turn my back to the TV and sign my displeasure during the maudlin scene where the boy is getting on the train and saying goodbye to his adoptive mother. "Oh honey, it's sad, I know it's a sad scene," Penny says. "Oh the sweet mother who adopted him, she's so sweet."

I know this movie has special meaning for her, so I try not to puke. Like I said, I've always thought of her as a sister—an annoying older sister—but over the years Penny has gradually come to see herself as my adoptive mother, my sweet adoptive mother, who also happens to be a scientist conducting an experiment on me.

Yes, Penny has made her peace with not having a baby, though not with *my* not having a baby. You can see it's complicated emotionally. My own feelings are complicated too. I never got too worked up over the baby thing. I mean, it either happens or it doesn't. But the value of this experiment in interspecies communication, the dream that all of those disgruntled employees bought into at one point or another—though Penny rarely let them near me and always monitored our interactions on closed circuit TV—I can't quite bring myself to deny it. Even if all Penny, Ron and I really are is one more dysfunctional American family, another crazy mom and checked-out dad eating junk food and watching TV in a broken down trailer alongside their lazy single adult child with a poor vocabulary—isn't there something to be learned from that?

Koko, the Voice of Nature

Lately people have been taking an interest in me again. This video, which Ron taped for the climate change conference in Paris, has earned the Gorilla Foundation website almost a million new hits. In the past four decades, I've had my fifteen minutes of fame—there was my bestselling children's book, *Koko's Kitten*, plus those televised visits from Mr. Rogers, Robin Williams and Leonardo DiCaprio. So it's not as if I were a total unknown, but this video has earned me a whole new following.

In the video, you see me signing: "I am gorilla, I am flowers, animals. I am Nature. Koko love man. Earth Koko love. But man stupid... stupid! Koko sorry, Koko cry. Time hurry. Fix Earth! Help Earth! Hurry! Protect Earth. Nature watches you. Thank you." Now I ask you, is this really what humans think Nature would say to them, if Nature had a voice? No expletives?

The disgruntled employees said all they really wanted from the Gorilla Foundation was honesty. They wished Penny would stop telling people she was going to open up the Maui preserve, stop telling them I was going to have a baby, and just make this simple pitch: "There's an aging gorilla in Woodside, California, condemned by a wayward science experiment to live her life out among humans, and she needs money to fix up her trailer." I'm fine with that—I'm all for honesty, as you know—except for the Woodside/trailer part. I'd actually prefer to live out my new, honest life in Maui.

And while we're on the subject of honesty, as much as I appreciate their concern, I think the disgruntled employees came down a bit too hard on the Foundation. Nowadays everyone thinks seventies environmentalism was so wrong-headed—no one today would *ever* think gorillas should live with humans, they say, rather than with each other, unmolested in the wild. But look what happened when you stopped obsessing over us, stopped feeding us Cheetos and cooked vegetables. You just started killing us. For fuck's sake, says the Voice of Nature, there are only eight hundred mountain gorillas left!

Koko Makes a Movie

But I don't want you to leave this website feeling deflated. Because I'm not just a critic, I'm also a maker. And I have a great idea for a movie of my own. Wouldn't you like to see a movie made by a gorilla? Picture this: me and Penny running hand and hand into the waves off Hamoa Beach—that's the beautiful crescent-shaped one on Maui—both of us naked, in a total state of nature. And Ron lumbering after us, also naked, his body and gait a lot like mine. Now that we're all stripped down, communing in paradise, these things can be acknowledged.

But then the camera pans to a speedboat anchored not far from where we frolic, revealing a troop of gorillas lounging on the deck in string bikinis and speedos, sipping on banana daiquiris and listening to the theme from Hawaii 5-0. I see them and freeze: the camera zooms in on my confused expression. I look back at Penny and Ron, and then from Ron and Penny to the gorillas on the speedboat—I'm so confused. Who am I? *What* am I? Where do I belong? And the title scrolls down the screen: *Meet Koko*.

I haven't gotten any further than the opening sequence, but you get the idea. This will be a story for the ages, folks—or the next age, anyway, the one where your salmon's laced with cocaine and anti-depressants, the bees have disappeared, and the clouds are seeded so you're never sure what or who's responsible for the rain. If you want to know what that's going to be like, if you're yearning to feel the shudder of recognition that attends a great work of art—if you're intrigued by the possibility that this artwork might come from a go-rilla, not a human, then hop on over to my crowdfunding page, more details await you there.

Monument

Every night at dusk we get into it. "That's it, it's done, I'm done, we're done," she says.

"Come on, get up," I say. "Look at that pile. Who's gonna notice it, not from out there, no way. Come on, get up. We're not done, not by a long shot. You got a headlamp, don't you?"

And she looks miserable at me for a long minute, then gets to her feet and switches on her little light.

The truth is, our pile's looking pretty good. We've been at it for weeks now, and there's a fairly tall stack of metal down there at the water's edge. But it's still not tall enough to be seen when the sun's not out, and you can't bet on their sailing by when it's sunny. Actually, you can bet on their *not* sailing by when it's sunny, because it's not sunny most of the time. Most of the time it's rain we're dealing with, a dirty, seeping rain that stings the hands and face. The lake water's poisoned too, always churning up dead fish and now and then a muddy pelican with a broken neck. But I try not to dwell on all that. I keep my mind on the pile.

"Even if they do see it," she grumbles, dusting the sand off her snow pants, "even if the sun's out and catches it just right—so what? They're not gonna stop."

This is another sticking point with my wife and me. Say that guy was right who passed through here, the old hippy with the ratty poncho and the stringy beard who kept grinning at her with his yellow teeth like I wasn't standing right next to her, say the rumor's true and rich people really are taking luxury cruises around the Great Lakes to gawk at the destruction, she has a hard time believing they might come ashore to inspect the pile, listen to our story and take us away with them. "Don't want their goddamn pity anyway," she says. "Why does it always come down to that, people like us begging for help from people like them?"

"Well, they're not gonna let you on their yacht with that mouth on you," I say.

We get into the golf cart, where we'll sleep later up on the boardwalk, and drive back to town, back to the auto parts store—or back to the place where the auto parts store used to be. It's our best find so far— we've been digging up mufflers and tailpipes for days. Before all this began, back when metal detecting was just a hobby, we used to look for small, special things, like antique jewelry, streetcar tokens, buffalo nickels, Barber dimes. Things of historical interest, stuff you could tell a story about. But now it's volume we're after. Volume and shine.

She sniffs and says, "We've already dug up all over that auto parts store," but she scoops up a handful of colored golf tees anyway and puts them in her pocket. Then she zips up her inside parka and her outside parka against the wind, pulls on her ski gloves and yanks down her hat. She suffers from the cold. But when the golf cart takes a turn and she slides into me, I can feel her body underneath all that padding and it stirs me and makes me mad at our situation all over again. "There's still plenty of parts in the ground if we can get to them," I say roughly.

She gives me a sharp look, then looks away.

I know she wants to go back to the bandstand. That's her favorite spot. Always was. Used to be for the things that fell out of people's pockets when they were lounging on the grass, now it's for the stuff kids left behind. A blue tin bucket, half-melted. A Western-style cap gun without a handle. One day she found a little Matchbox car that was magically preserved. "Honey, look!" she said, holding it up like we were shopping for Christmas presents. We spent an hour digging up the mangled red tricycle that's now at the heart of the pile.

"No more," I said at the end of that day. "No more of this, okay?"

But I want to get to the bottom of the auto parts. I can't believe how much metal there still is in this little town, under all that ash. She gets the machine out of the back of the cart and sets off, and I zip up my parkas and retrieve the pick axe and the shovel, giving her time to plant the brightly colored tees that tell me where to dig. A good two hours and six rearview mirrors, twelve hubcaps and what looks to be one carburetor later, we remember we're hungry. That's what I've always loved about metal detecting—you enter a kind of deep time that's hard to come back from. Because unlike people and places, metal lasts. It may be rusted or twisted beyond recognition, but it lasts.

She's fired up now and wants to keep going because she knows after we eat it'll be my turn with the machine and hers with the pick-axe and the shovel, but I remind her how important it is to keep up our strength. So we get in the cart and head for the underground vault that's been in my family for generations—as long as the creaky wooden house that once stood over it—which is where we keep our foodstuffs and water now.

Driving through the ash, I have a hard time believing here once stood a town like ours, with a friendly little post office and a falling down school and a line of boarded up storefronts. It's even harder to believe that beyond the town there were white dunes with green dune grass and beyond the dune grass a wide, sandy beach and a big blue lake that was clean enough most days to swim in. I'm not sure I do believe it anymore, and I know she doesn't. When you stop believing in your memories they become a kind of dream.

Oh, we almost got out, we did get out, we evacuated with the kids in plenty of time, but it was our bad luck—ours and a whole bunch of other people's—that one of those deadly viruses burned through the camp within twenty-four hours. But you don't want to hear that story. To be honest, I only remember the very end, when I found the golf cart and drove it back to camp and carried her out to it half-alive.

She's the one who notices that the dirt and ash we always cover up the vault with have been displaced and the lock's been tampered with. "Somebody's been banging at it trying to get in," she says, and when I tell her she's imagining things she says, "Look!" and points to the scratches.

"An animal was here," I say. "A raccoon maybe."

"Uh huh. When was the last time you saw a raccoon?"

"Well, they didn't get in, whoever it was. They won't get in, that's a high security lock."

"Yes," she says. "But who?"

"The more important question is how? How did they know it was even down there?"

Her eyes light up. "I'll bet it was someone from the Club," she hisses, and I can see her body go rigid with indignation, even through all those layers.

"Aw, come on, be real. You really think there's somebody else out here with a metal detector?"

"Think it," she says. "I know it. I'll bet it's Charlie Ross."

"Why Charlie Ross?"

"Because he's just weasel enough to steal our food."

She's had it in for Charlie ever since he challenged me for president of the Diggers Club and then took half the club with him when he didn't win. But I didn't blame him. People were out of work, they'd lost interest in the historical dimension. All they cared about was finding jewelry and change—stuff that would put food on their table.

"Get in," she says, taking the wheel of the cart. "We're going for a ride."

"So long as it ends up back here," I shrug. "I'm hungry."

She steps on the accelerator and even though the cart is solar-powered and like I said there's not much sunlight these days she gets it going at a pretty fast clip. Soon we're careening all over the place because let's face it, she's never been a good driver, added to the fact that we're off-roading in a golf cart, but she's sure somebody's out there, so we have to circle round and round for hours until whatever daylight there was is gone and we're charging at shapes in the dark.

"Hey," I say finally. "Hey."

At first I don't think she hears me but the cart eventually comes to a stop and then she's just sitting there, staring into the darkness. I turn to look at her and my headlamp lights up the tears sliding down her cheeks. "Hey," I say. "Let me drive."

And then she's back at it with the nobody's ever going to come we're going to die here I wish I'd died when the kids did I wish we'd both died then and gotten it over with what kind of monsters outlive their children, but she gets out as she's talking and I move over and she climbs back in on the other side. I start up the cart and head back to the vault to pick up some MREs to eat on our way out to the beach, but she won't touch hers.

When we get there, she sits in the cart on the boardwalk while I unload the auto parts and take them down to the water's edge. I stack the big pieces carefully and place the mirrors all around to reflect the light from every angle when it comes. The pile's starting to take shape now, a tower-shape that looks purposeful even though it's not, a shape that makes you want to get closer, close enough to understand, or at least that's what I'm hoping.

I go back up and try to talk to her but she's still slumped over staring straight ahead with those empty eyes. "Well, good night sweetie," I say. "It'll all look better in the morning." I get in beside her and put my feet up on the dash and pull my hat down low over my face to keep out the rain that drives in under the canopy, but it's hours before I can sleep and that whole time she sits perfectly still, eyes staring and staring.

Next thing I know she's hammering at me with her elbow. "Wake up, damn you, wake up!"

I open my eyes and it's still dark but the rain has stopped and there's a light coming from offshore, a searchlight sweeping the beach and landing on the pile, going up and down and all around it. Suddenly I'm wide awake and we're running down to the water's edge, both of us screaming "We're here! We're here!" which isn't something we'd agreed upon to scream, it's just what comes out of us as we're running toward the pile, trying to get to there in time to be seen. And we're laughing, we're racing, we're shrieking with joy—it's as if we're the children and they're the parents who've come back for us.

When the light switches off and leaves us alone on the shore, she doesn't say a word, just falls to her knees and then her face in the sand, and I fall right down next to her and wail like a baby—loud, ugly, shaking sobs. I haven't cried once this whole goddamn time, you understand, not even when they came with the bags to take our kids away.

"Well, now you know what that sounds like," I say after a while, rolling onto my back, and I feel something soft land on my chest, a hand in a ski glove—her hand in her ski glove—but before I can clutch it, before I can press it to my lips, before I can unzip her outer parka and her inner parka and feel her flesh against mine, alive, alive, she rolls away.

When I wake up in the morning on the cold hard sand and she's gone it's no surprise, in fact it takes me a little while to react because it makes such perfect sense—deep down I can't believe she waited this long. But then I wake all the way up and scramble to my feet to scan the beach. The sun's broken through the clouds for the first time in weeks and my eyes have a hard time focusing—everything looks different in the bright harsh light. I scan the lake, too, because that's how she always said she would end it, but there's no sign of her anywhere, the beach is empty except for our gleaming pile of junk, that shining monument to foolish hope. And it makes me so stupidly mad I run over and kick it, and kick it again, because who cares, who cares, now that she's gone, but when one of the rearview mirrors falls down I pick it up out of habit and put it back where it belongs.

I turn around, nursing my foot, and that's when I spot her, a tiny round figure in the distance. She's walking towards me down the beach, waving the machine from side to side in a slow steady sweep, with the kind of control that takes years of practice to perfect. Lost in deep time, she doesn't see me wave or hear me call, so I go back to the cart for the long handled scoop and make my way up to greet her.

The Protester Has Been Released

He Chooses to Join

He hadn't planned on joining the protest. He'd been interested, that's all. Interested in the signs scattered around the periphery, in the library they'd set up in a tent, in the classes on offer out on the lawn. Interested in the smell of bacon—where was it coming from? And was it real bacon or the vegetarian kind? The guy peddling a stationary bike to power the laptops—now that was interesting, wasn't it?

That he should be holding a sign when the cops showed up, that he should suddenly be flanked by protesters holding signs behind and beside him—that was all happenstance. But that he should join in their chant, that he should stick around even after being told to leave, that he should link arms with the protesters, becoming a protester himself—well, that his was choice.

The Protester Meets Officer Pike

Soon after becoming a protester, he met a chaotic individual named Officer Pike. They met when Officer Pike ripped the sign out of his hands and tore it in half. "Hey!" the Protester said, and Officer Pike pepper-sprayed him. "My eyes!" the Protester screamed, and Officer

Pike whirled him around and handcuffed him. "Could we just talk about this?" the Protester shrieked, and Officer Pike finally spoke. "You're under arrest, asshole," he said, to the back of the Protester's head.

The Protester Has Been Released

The Protester has been released on bail after a few hours in custody, along with many other protesters. His wife picks him up outside the jail and they ride home on a wave of relief. They think it's over.

The Protester Has Assaulted an Officer

At his arraignment, the Protester learns he has assaulted an officer. "What?" he blurts out. "How?" The Public Defender apologizes profusely for the disruption.

The District Attorney Reads Aloud From Officer Pike's Report

"I sustained multiple injuries while taking the perpetrator into custody: a paper cut on the left hand, as well as muscle strain in the neck and forearms."

The Defense

Despite the Protester's outburst and Officer Pike's damning report, the Public Defender is confident he can get the charges dismissed. Smilingly, he tells the D.A. and the judge the Protester is not the man they think he is. He's not even a real protester—he's just a cabinetmaker, a young father who got swept up by events. As he looks around the courtroom, the Public Defender's voice trails off. No one's convinced. Somebody must be made to answer for the paper cut. Those things hurt!

The Protesters Take the Bridge

The arraignment is over; the Protester's case will go to trial. He hails a taxi outside the courthouse and goes to pick his daughter up from daycare. As the taxi reaches the bridge, traffic stops, and a river of protesters rushes through the stilled cars as if a dam has broken.

Of course the Protester thinks their cause is just, but right now he wishes they weren't holding up traffic because he has to get his daughter from daycare. His wife has asked him to do this one little thing—could he just do this one little thing? He exits the taxi and begins walking across the bridge in the opposite direction of the protest. He can get another taxi on the other side.

For what seems like a long time, he weaves his way through the protesters weaving through the cars, until, halfway across, he finds himself alone in the middle of six empty lanes. Now late to pick up his daughter, he keeps going. As he passes the bridge's massive tension cables and hears the water crashing against the pylons many feet below, he experiences a dizzying sensation of freedom. Too late, he sees the line of police cars rolling towards him, lights silently flashing.

The Protester looks over the railing. But he can't, he can't.

The Protester's Wife Has Not Recovered

The Protester's wife still hasn't recovered from his first arrest. She wakes up in the middle of the night, heart pounding. More often than he, she wakes.

A Man Sits in His Car

A man sits in his car on the bridge, watching the protesters. He's had his own run-ins with the law and feels no urge to join them.

A Woman Sits in Her Car

A woman sits in her car on the bridge, thinking how marvelous. How marvelous that people are finally rising up to say something. How marvelous that they're disrupting business as usual. Thank you! she shouts inside her car, deafening herself—and then, rolling down her window, thank you! I'll sit here all day if it comes to that, she thinks, rolling the window back up (it's a little chilly outside). This is what democracy looks like, she thinks, smiling at the protesters. They don't smile back. Not great PR, but still, she supports them. Her fingers drum the steering wheel.

Another Man Sits in His Car

Another man sits in his car on the bridge thinking, this is one of those change-your-life moments, like in that Rilke poem. He doesn't.

The Protester Uses His App

The Protester uses his I'm-being-arrested-app to notify his wife that he's being arrested again. She stares at her phone in disbelief. Luckily her office is not far away from their daughter's daycare. She can't think any further ahead than that.

His Lawyer Doesn't Understand

"So you weren't protesting," his new lawyer says slowly. He's a private attorney, not a Public Defender. "You were just walking across the bridge."

The Protester nods.

"I don't understand. In the middle of a protest?"

The Protester shrugs. Nobody believes him. Nobody believes any of the guys on his cellblock, who are all serving time for things they didn't do. He didn't believe them either at first, but now he's starting to. He's starting to believe they just happened to be in the wrong place at the wrong time, standing next to the real perpetrator, or right behind him. It's very easy to be in the wrong place at the wrong time, he realizes. Before he thought it took more of an effort.

The Protester Feels Like One of Them

"Officer Pike," they nod. "He booked my little brother." Officer Pike has seemingly booked all of their little brothers, and for what? Cursing at Officer Pike. Riding past Officer Pike on a scooter. Looking Officer Pike in the eye. He has booked their mothers and grandmothers, too, for refusing to turn them in. Himself unjustly charged, the Protester feels like one of them. He's not one of them.

The Protester is Out Again

The Protester is out again on bail and spending the day with his daughter. While walking to the library, they spot several protesters hanging a banner on the stock exchange and stop to watch. The protesters, wearing black balaclavas, shimmy up and down on bungee cords anchored to the roof of the skyscraper. "Spiders!" his daughter cries out, pointing her chubby finger, and the Protester shudders.

The Protester Has Wild Dreams

The night before his trial for felony assault of a police officer, the Protester has wild dreams. In the first, most satisfying dream, a tearful Officer Pike recants his testimony and begs the Protester and his wife for forgiveness, which they stolidly refuse. In the second, the Judge sentences the Protester to a life of solitude, pounding his gavel so hard the bench crumbles to the floor in a cloud of dust, exposing its termite-riddled insides. In the third dream, a team of balaclava-clad protesters forces their way into the courtroom and attaches a bungee cord to the Protester. They rush him over to the window and yell, "Jump!" But he can't, he can't.

The Protesters Are on an Island

Student protesters have converged on an island in the middle of a major thoroughfare near campus and are waving their signs at honking cars. As more students arrive, they spill out into the street. Traffic slows. This means the protest is a success. News trucks arrive. This means the protest is even more successful. Traffic stops. This means the protest is over.

When traffic stops, the protest ends and the anti-protest begins. Riot cops appear on the horizon like a great insect migration, in their segmented black vests, clear visors, clicking boots and huge numbers. They circle the island and close in, using their shields to move the students back up onto the curb and into the decorative cacti. The students look around for reinforcements. If only there were more of them.

The Bill From the Lawyer

The Protester cannot show his wife the bill from the lawyer. He shows his wife the bill. His wife cannot speak. "I feel sick," she says.

The Protester Is Very Lucky

In the big scheme of things, the Protester is very lucky. He's lucky to be spearing trash by the side of the highway in a bright yellow shirt. Luckily, he only has a hundred and twenty more hours to go. Considering his crimes—the paper cut, the muscle strain, crossing a vehicular bridge on foot—he got off easy.

The Protester stabs at a milk carton, feeling sad and alone and broke. He should be radicalized by what he's gone through, but frankly he doesn't know if he will ever protest again. His wife encourages him to follow his conscience, lending her troubled support, but they're just two little people, taking care of an even littler person. His friends voice their admiration, but he can tell they think it's time to stop. "Leave it to the next generation," one of them says, slapping him on the back. "You're a family man now."

It's a hot day, and the Protester stops to mop his brow. It's then that he spots the swarm approaching, the locusts released by the student protesters earlier in the day, increasing their numbers by the millions. At the sight of the insect cloud, the rest of the highway beautification crew runs to the truck, but the Protester is oddly unafraid. He stands still and waits, arms by his sides, palms turned upward. In less than a minute, the locusts have landed all over his body, thrumming their iridescent wings, a righteous infestation that cannot be contained.

Sunshine Collective

Dear Sarah,

It was great meeting you at Irene's Thanksgiving and I really appreciate your interest in my work. I'm emailing as we discussed to set up a meeting—next week is pretty open for me.

Looking forward,
Pieter

Dear Sarah,

I was wondering if you still wanted to meet up? I'm free on Monday night, if that works for you.

All best,
Pieter

Dear Sarah,

Happy New Year! Hope your holidays were great. I was wondering if you might have some time in the next week for that meeting?

Yours,
Pieter

Dear Sarah,

I hope you're doing great. For me, it's been an insanely busy couple of months! I founded an art collective called Arcosanti in January and we've got a ton of events planned. Was wondering if you might want to sit down and chat about the new work. Lots going on!

Yours,
Pieter

Peter,

Can you meet me at the Mandrake today at 5?

Sarah

...Oh no, Sarah! Can't believe I missed your email! I was offline, working with the collective on a composting toilet/computer desk. How about tomorrow? Breakfast?

Dear Sarah,

I'm kicking myself for missing your email last week! Still up for a meeting if you are.

Pieter

Dear Sarah,

Just saw the good news on FB! Congratulations! The Museum is lucky to have you.

All best,
Pieter

Peter,

I hope things have been going well for you and the Sunshine Collective. I'm in charge of summer programming for the Museum and I wanted to see if you guys might be interested in activating a space for us. Let me know as soon as possible.

Sarah

Dear Sarah,

Great to hear from you after all this time—we're interested! The name of our collective though is *Arcosanti*, named for Paolo Soleri's utopian ecological project in the Arizona desert. Our interactive artworks and participatory events encourage people to explore the environmental effects of computer technology—would you like me to send you an artist statement? Oh, and it's Pieter, not Peter.

All best,
Pieter

Peter,

Where did I get "Sunshine Collective"? Were you ever called the Sunshine Collective?

Sarah

Dear Sarah,

Nope, and neither was anybody else—I googled it.

All best,
Pieter

Peter,

I'm thinking about a summer residency with you guys doing four or five events in the space. How does that sound?

Sarah

Dear Sarah,

That sounds amazing. Is the space in the Museum itself, or off-site?

Pieter

Peter,

It's in the Museum proper. Can I send over the paperwork? We can sort out the exact dates later. You wouldn't believe how many events I'm expected to put on—they want me to activate the entire Museum from top to bottom.

Sarah

Dear Sarah,

Sure, but just wondering—is there a budget?

Pieter

Peter,

There's a small honorarium, and we'll pay for refreshments and help with the cost of materials.

Sarah

Dear Sarah,

Super! Send over the paper work! And just a reminder for the forms: it's Pieter, not Peter.

Pieter

Dear Sarah,

Was wondering if you got the signed contract I faxed you last week? And if so, how we should proceed? Do you want to try to hammer out the dates over email? Should we come take a look at the space? Can't wait!

Pieter

Peter,

I'm traveling at the moment with spotty Internet—let's talk when I get back to LA!

Sarah

Dear Sarah,

I was on the west side today with a couple of my Arcosanti collaborators and we stopped in at the museum to take a look at the summer residency space. The lady at the front desk drew a blank at first, but when I mentioned your name it clicked. She showed us a long dark hallway leading to the staff restroom. That can't be right, can it?

All best,
Pieter

Peter,

Patty said you'd been by. Shoot, I wanted to clear the boxes out first. If ever a space needed activating, it's that one, right? I was thinking you might want to install some of your composting toilet/computer desks down there. I mean, just on display, not for people to actually use. But there's a thematic tie-in, for sure.

Sarah

Dear Sarah,

First of all, because Arcosanti works deliberately slowly, there's only one composting toilet/computer desk. Like Soleri, who refused corporate sponsorship for the construction of his utopian desert community, preferring to rely solely on student and hippy labor, we would rather do it right than do it quickly. We're aware that in the case of Soleri's Arcosanti, this resulted in Phase 1 buildings falling into ruin before Phases 2 and 3 could be completed, but we respect that. It would take us the entire summer to complete another toilet/desk.

And secondly, who exactly are we activating the space for? Patty said the only people allowed access to that hallway are staff. Sorry, I'm just confused.

Pieter

Peter,

I know it's not a typical museum space—but isn't that what makes it interesting? Also, I'm sure you didn't mean to come across like this, but are you saying staff members don't deserve to experience art? A staff Museum event still counts as a Museum event (for me *and* for you).

Sarah

Dear Sarah,

Arcosanti held a long meeting last night where we really thrashed out our issues with the space plus our latent elitism towards our audience. It was super-productive and I'm glad to say we're ready to move forward with our Museum residency and we'll be happy to install our one existing toilet/computer desk in the hallway. Needless to say, your arguments were very convincing. Can I just say how much I value our back and forth? This is why I make art, to challenge and be challenged.

Pieter

Peter,

Glad to hear it. And good news—it looks like you'll have seven summer interns!

Sarah

Dear Sarah,

I'm writing to let you know how our first event went and also to relay a concern. The interns were really helpful clearing the boxes out of the hallway and installing the composting toilet/computer desk. They also made for a very appreciative audience once the event got started and were game to participate in our trust-fall-over-a-pile-of-e-waste exercise. So all in all, I would say it was a successful evening. The only issue was that no paid staff attended, since they left the Museum promptly at 5, and it doesn't seem like they're going to want to attend any of the other evening events we had planned. Would it be possible to reschedule those for lunchtime?

Best,
Pieter

Dear Sarah,

Reporting back on our second event, which took place during lunch and attracted a really good crowd! We went around the room and introduced ourselves, so I have a pretty clear picture of who came: the entire Facilities crew and most of Security, a few ladies from Finance and a couple of guys from IT. No one showed up from Curatorial or Education, which was a little disappointing, but there's always next time! We gave a presentation on our composting toilet/computer desk project to those in attendance, which folks seemed very interested in and weirdly angry about. Turns out a rumor had been circulating that Admin was planning to install composting toilet/computer desks in the staff restroom to reduce the Museum's carbon footprint and boost productivity. And they thought we were there to conduct a training session on how to use them!

"Oh, this thing doesn't even work!" we assured them, and everybody had a big laugh. "That's what makes it art, right?" one of the security guards called out and we all had an even bigger laugh. Then the accountants wanted to know how much we were getting paid to hang out there in the hallway with our nonfunctioning toilet/desk and—full disclosure here—I told them. "How do you make a living doing what you do?" asked one of the groundskeepers, but before we could answer somebody asked him, "How do you make a living doing what *you* do?" And after that there was a good discussion about salaries at the Museum and hierarchies of labor and other forms of social organization that aren't hierarchical, like artist collectives. Everyone said they really enjoyed the event, and somebody suggested we would get an even bigger crowd next time if we ordered pizza. I love the way these collaborations unfold!

Yours,
Pieter

Peter,

God, I always hate this moment—the moment when you guys ask for more money and I have to tell you there is none, absolutely none, and how I wish things were different. Given our limited resources, we try to support as many artists as possible, rather than directing all our funding to just a lucky few. I hope, being a collective, you'll understand.

Best,
Sarah

Dear Sarah,

I wasn't actually asking for more money—things are going great. Though from the discussion I had with Museum staff, it sounds like all the funding *is* being directed to just a lucky few, those lucky few just happen to be administrators.

All best,
Pieter

Peter,

Today I received a $600 bill from a sushi restaurant. Can you explain? This is way out of the realm of refreshments.

Sarah

Dear Sarah,

What an incredible event we had yesterday! It was just going to be a pizza party, as I mentioned in my last email, but then when everybody got there and we were about to order, one of the security guards shouted out, "Fuck pizza! I want sushi!" and the cry went around the room, and then someone from IT yelled, "I want what those Google motherfuckers get on their lunch hour! I want a massage!" So there's a bill for that on its way to you, too. But the best part came when we were all sitting in a circle talking about how technology and nature intersected in our own lives, and how technology isn't just high tech but all the ways we have of acting upon our environment, and somebody had the awesome idea to cut a hole in the ceiling so the hallway wouldn't be so dark and we could all look up at the sky. And none of them had ever seen a Turrell! I guess you got your Sunshine Collective after all!

All best,
Pieter

Peter,

With this email I'm terminating Arcosanti's residency at the Museum. I'll be putting your honorarium towards the cost of repairing the ceiling, the sushi et al.

Sarah

Dear Sarah,

Oh no! You can't be serious? I thought things were going really well. I mean, people stayed until five o'clock yesterday! Even some supervisors came down near the end, to see where everybody was, and that was the first time any of them had ever been in that space. Please reconsider!

All best,
Pieter

Dear Sarah,

Arcosanti had a long meeting last night where we reflected on our residency at the Museum, and I wanted to share our findings with you. Despite the fact that it was abruptly curtailed, we honestly think a lot of good work came out of our time there—not least of all, the ceiling cut, which we thankfully managed to document before it was destroyed. And the rapport we built up with our audience in the course of just three events was amazing—we learned so much from them and we think they learned a few things from us, too. They may think a little differently now about the relationship between nature and technology, but more importantly they think differently about *art*, and who it's for, and I dare say they think it might be for them. So in our book, that all counts as a big success.

On the topic of exceeding our budget there were mixed opinions, but ultimately we agreed we could've handled that more professionally. Of course, if Turrell went over budget nobody would bat an eyelash, right? But the standards for the kind of art we do seem to be different, which is something the Museum may want to think about.

Overall, though, everyone was open to collaborating with you again in the future. I hope now that a little time has passed, the value of our project to the Museum has offset the cost in your eyes.

All best,
Pieter

Peter,

Your toilet thing is out on the loading dock. You need to pick it up by tomorrow at 5 or it's going in the trash.

Sarah

Dear Sarah,

Don't you mean the recycling? Just kidding. We'll get it first thing tomorrow morning.

All best,
Pieter

Dear Sarah,

You definitely missed out on some craziness at the Museum yesterday, but I want you to know it wasn't as crazy as they probably told you it was. We were merely planning to pick up the toilet/desk and then stop by your office to say thanks on our way out, but as we were loading it into the truck some of the guys from Facilities stopped to chat and then I guess the news spread like wildfire that our residency had been terminated, because by the time we got up to your office only to be told you were out for the day, a big crowd had formed around us. Somebody—not one of us—shouted, "We want to see the Executive Director!" and we were saying "No! no! we just want to get out of here," but it was too late, we were swept up by the crowd and carried down the hall into the Executive Director's office.

The E.D. came around his desk and his hands were shaking, which was kind of hard to believe, but I guess when you're so outnumbered plus you know you're underpaying your employees, it makes you tremble. "What are your demands?" he asked, and somebody said, "We want raises!" But then somebody else yelled, "Fuck raises! We want to run this Museum as a self-organizing COLLECTIVE!" and everyone shouted "YEAH!" The E.D looked like he was about to pass out, but when Patty whispered something in his ear he calmed down. "Sure, let's talk about it!" he said, going back behind his desk. "And how about some pizza?" On our way out, after the pizza, I asked Patty what she'd said to him, and she said she just told him it was an art piece.

So, though I hope the Museum does become a self-organizing collective—and would be very happy to be a part of that!—I wanted to let you know that was not our intention in dropping by your office.

We only wanted to thank you for the opportunity.

All best,
Pieter

Dear Sarah,

Congratulations on getting through your summer programming! I'm checking in to see how the Museum is planning to document all that great work, including the Arcosanti residency. I've got some stellar photos of the ceiling cut and would be happy to send them along.

All best,
Pieter

Dear Sarah,

I was so happy to see Arcosanti mentioned in the catalogue—however briefly! I wanted to point out though that you misspelled my name, just in case there's another printing.

All best,
Pieter

Ars Longa

Zoe

My father founded the Institute the year everyone got cancer. My mother first and then there was the boy on the college swim team, the one all his buddies shaved their heads for in solidarity, except then they all got cancer and there was no more swim team and no one to shave their heads in solidarity because by then pretty much everyone in town had it. Hairlessness was the new normal as were walkers and canes and people throwing up in garbage cans. They tried getting the EPA out to see if it was just our town but the EPA said no, it wasn't just our town, plus their field agents all had cancer and the one for our region was neutropenic and unable to travel.

When one person falls sick, they start down their own, lonely timeline, absenting themselves from work and other group activities, but when everyone is sick, really sick, the car goes off the rails. Meetings stop. Classes stop. Buses run empty, then don't run at all. You can't count on anyone being in the right place at the right time, or there even being a right place and a right time. The only place keeping to a schedule now is the hospital. The town square is empty save for abandoned dogs and cats, the shops on Main Street are all boarded up except the pharmacy, but when you step through the doors of the old Victorian brick hospital, with its loopy gingerbread façade, everybody's there.

If you didn't know any better, you might think my family has a special connection to that hospital. There's an oil painting of my mother's grandfather, the bank president, at the entrance, and another one in the atrium of her great grandfather, the governor. They were both benefactors. But it's no more special than our connection to the library, or the college or the Elks lodge. The Pitkins have been benefacting this town ever since they ran the Utes out of Colorado, though my branch of the family has never seen any of that largesse. My mother, an only child, was disowned by her parents for marrying my father, a Greek, who ran a popular diner on Main Street that was a thumb in their eye till the end of their days.

He's the only one in our family who doesn't have cancer, which is how he had the energy to found an art school, I guess. I never knew he was fond of art nor had any interest in it at all, although like all Greeks he studies the Ancients in his spare time. He didn't go to college, but he always had a dog-eared copy of Aristotle sitting on the back of the toilet at home. "In all things of nature, there's something of the marvelous," he liked to say upon exiting the can.

Since we had been to college, he decided my older brothers and I should be the ones to design and run the Institute, though Spyros was the only one with a degree in the arts—a double major in music and dance, my insanely talented brother. The dance part had always needled my father, but now that everyone has cancer he no longer seems to care. My own degree is in communications, but it doesn't really matter what degree a girl gets, so long as she finds a good husband (and even if I don't find a good husband, that's okay with him now, too, because cancer). The plan was that Spyros would co-chair the music and dance departments, I would oversee visual art (because communication), and my oldest brother George, with his business degree, would head up the theater program, a job for which his main qualifications were a line of failed startups and an explosive temper.

He'd been furious that Dad hadn't wanted to make the Institute a for-profit art school—he had a business plan all worked up, but per usual my father dismissed his idea. "You don't go to college to learn business," he's always telling George, "you start a business to learn business." But this time his response really cut to the quick: "For profit for who?" he scoffed. "You kids aren't going to be around much longer and neither am I."

That was hard to hear and my brother stormed off, but at the same time it was somehow freeing. Like we didn't even have to charge tuition for our school, because we weren't going to live long enough to need the money. And our students wouldn't have to worry about loans or finding a job after graduation, because same. The best time to found an art school seems to be when things are either really good or when they're terrible.

"Is anyone even going to want to come?" Spyros said, tying his fuzzy little warm up jacket tighter around his waspish waist. That's the kind of gesture that used to drive my father crazy, but now he doesn't even notice.

"Make it interesting, and you'll see."

Spyros gave him a cool look. "Oh, so now you *want* us to be interesting."

But we did make it interesting, and they did come. We took over a whole wing of the hospital, the one devoted to diseases other than cancer, which was now empty. That meant that all they (or we) had to do to get to the Institute from the treatment center was cross the courtyard, which they (we) did all day long, shuttling back and forth between art and chemo. The hospital architecture was well suited to our needs: wide corridors for carting around equipment and sets; whole floors reconfigurable into dance studios, practice rooms and ateliers; a grassy hillside for the amphitheater Dad was planning to build; and a chapel, which is where my mother was.

We didn't make a distinction between faculty and students—why bother? There wasn't time to apprentice or professionalize, there was barely time to make anything, or even think of anything to make. We just invited people to come. It's that way at the hospital now too, with the medical staff and the patients—all hierarchies are gone. We sit around adjusting each other's IVs and trading remedies for constipation, adrift on a sea of shock and confusion. They say a team is working on the cure over at the university, that all around the country, scientists are working on the cure, but haven't they always been working on the cure?

Costa

It's a Greek tragedy we're living through, but it's brought my children home, and for that, like any Greek father would be—except maybe Oedipus's—I'm grateful. For them, though, it's chaos. Their mother dying, as hard as that was, was still within the order of things. But what about their future? George, that numbskull—I always thought he'd take over the diner once he burned through those business school ideas, but the diner's closed, I had to shut it down. Who's eating diner food? The very thought of it makes them sick, George most of all.

He has that wildfire kind of cancer, the kind that burns through your body so fast they don't even know where it started. Metastatic Carcinoma of Unknown Primary Origin, they call it, or Good Luck Sonny You're on Your Own. He's a big boy, but this thing is hollowing him out. My daughter's disease started in her womb, slowly, they tell us, but it had spread all over her belly by the time they caught it. No one was looking for cancer, not in a twenty-something, and not in all of them, all at once. It's hard to believe, but Spyros is the strongest of the three; it's in his lungs and his liver but you would never know.

Like everyone else, in the beginning I struggled to understand, to find a way to help. How did the Ancients cope with chaos? I wondered during those sleepless nights, and found the answer in Aristotle, as usual: by giving it form—by making art. That's something I can still give my children, I thought to myself, the opportunity to make art. And then I thought, hell, why only my kids, why not the whole town?

Since I'm an upstanding citizen and a respected businessman, the Hospital agreed to let us use the empty wing for the Institute, if I would manage the cafeteria. And though managing a hospital cafeteria full of cancer patients is even less rewarding than running a diner, I'm content, because my children are a part of something beautiful. As Aristotle said, the quality of a life is determined by its activities. Plus, I get to dig out an amphitheater in my spare time, and that's worthwhile. I need to do something with my strength, it's obscene how strong I am, how good my color is. People stare at me in disgust as I'm walking through the hospital.

Spyros

The day the Institute opened and we stood in the doorway watching our first enrollees wheel, crutch and cane themselves across the courtyard—that was a good day. Never thought the old Neanderthal had it in him to pull it off. Of course, I also watched them with a heavy heart, because how was I supposed to make those bodies dance and sing? I was a professional, I could push myself, and my cancer hadn't yet spread beyond a couple of organs. But those sad specimens—how were they to dance? How were they to make music, with the hours of practice that entails? Then again, seen from another angle they were dancing already, hobbling and jerking across the courtyard. And the cacophony of their equipment—that was a kind of music, wasn't it?

No, the hardest part of teaching at the Institute was going to be working every day alongside my nerdy sister, moody brother and the Neanderthal. I mean, wasn't that why I became a dancer, why I taught myself fifteen instruments, why I moved to New York—to get away from all of them? But when M'Lady got sick and made her exit from this fucked up planet, leaving it a lesser place—and our family an even less hospitable environment for yours truly—I came back to be with her and got stuck here with my own diagnosis. Our hospital is one of the best cancer hospitals around, which is saying something considering how many are around.

And to be honest, the epidemic has loosened things up a lot. Everyone's a little more willing to try stuff, a little less worried about what it *says* about who they *are*. There's an eros to our situation: the orderlies at the hospital, the mailman, even the salesman at the one remaining shoe store in town, where I bought my first wingtips as a boy—they're ready to romp. What's there to lose? I'd fuck all day if it weren't for the Institute.

George

I just treated the theater program like any other startup. On the very first day, I said to them, "We're going to brainstorm while we're waiting for my dad to dig out the amphitheater; we're going to get to know each other with trust exercises, journaling and reciprocal massages. And then I want to hear from you what you want to do. I'm not going to pick our first show. *You're* going to pick it. What's it going to be? A musical? A drama? A comedy? A dramady? All ideas welcome."

We had a good vibe going, morale was high, more than one person came down on the side of musical theater, we talked it out. "Let's keep it light," they said. "Forget about the sad stuff for a while. For two hours, let's take our audience on a whole other journey."

"Ugh," the haters responded. "To a land where people spontaneously break out into song? Rouge our pallid cheeks? Wear long blonde wigs? Aren't we beyond the aesthetics of denial?"

One of them suggested Greek theater. "Well, that would make my father happy," I said.

"But so depressing if we don't achieve a full catharsis," said another. "Plus, didactic."

"I've got it!" said someone else. "How about cabaret—last days, Weimar Republic style? *Cabaret!* We can all don fishnet stockings and be lewd and political!"

Everyone looked thoughtful. "It is the last days," said a small voice in the back, "but what's to be gotten out of skewering our politicians?"

"Ah yes," someone muttered. "Cancer, the great equalizer."

"It's not that they don't deserve to be skewered," said the small voice. "It's just not that satisfying."

And then the nurse stood up. I recognized her from the treatment center; she's a good nurse. A beautiful nurse with coal black eyes—I think she's a Ute.

"What if we were to get on stage and just ask questions?" she said, looking around the room. "Don't you all have a lot of questions?"

Zoe

My mother and I have always been close, but since she's had a chance to reflect on her life, she has so much to tell me. She's full of wisdom now about what it means to be a woman in a man's world.

"Beauty," she pronounces as soon as I enter the chapel, "is something women deal with their whole lives: having it, not having it, having had it, not having had it, wanting it, wanting to have had it or someday still to have it. There is, after all, such a thing as a handsome older woman, though nine times out of ten she was also a beautiful young girl."

"Children," she goes on, "are a very serious thing. I didn't believe that until I had one. As a young woman, the seriousness of children seemed like a ruse to keep me from following my dreams. But you listen to me, Zoe: children *are* serious. They can kill you. They can die."

And then there's the sweet spot. "As you grow older, your powers will diminish, but your wisdom will increase. There's a sweet spot where your powers and wisdom are just about equal, but usually you can only identify it in retrospect, and have squandered it on getting your teenagers into college. Be on the lookout for your sweet spot.

Do something big with it."

I ask why she never mentored me before.

"I was too busy trying to keep you alive."

"But I probably won't live long enough now to put these lessons into practice."

"Nonsense. You're going to be fine."

I tell her I slept with a guy last night. And a different guy this morning. She's surprised, this isn't like me—I'm shy, I wear glasses and used to carry around an extra ten pounds to keep the world at bay. I'm a watcher, not a doer, and certainly not that kind of doer. But everywhere I go nowadays, somebody's looking at me with puppy dog eyes. The hospital frowns on our behavior but the supply closets are hopping. Oh to be young, horny and dying, with access to a full array of pharmaceuticals!

My mother's silent for so long I'm afraid she's gone away. "Are you at least using contraception?" she asks finally.

Costa

So here I make George a beautiful amphitheater, with stone seats and a view of the Rockies all around, and all he can think of to perform there is QUESTIONS?

"I thought you'd be happy," he tells me. "Think of it as philosophy."

"I don't want philosophy, I want theater. I was hoping for Oedipus Rex."

"Why that one?"

"The curse, of course—the plague ravaging Thebes. Don't you see the parallels?"

"Well, that's not the direction we're taking. We're going with the nurse's idea."

That pisses me off. "Stop sniffing around that nurse," I say. "She's a Ute, she wants nothing to do with you."

"Oh really? What do you know?"

I know a lot, actually. I work closely with the Utes. I buy all the produce for the hospital cafeteria from them. As other supply sources have dwindled, I've come to rely on them more and more. The Utes aren't sick, so they're the only ones growing anything around here. They bring what they grow, and I buy whatever they bring, so we're basically eating the traditional Ute diet now: amaranth, wild onion, rice grass, dandelion. I'm secretly hoping this will make my customers well. Sanpitch is the one I deal with mostly; the nurse is his daughter, Chipeta. What do you know? my son says to me. I know a lot.

Spyros

I usually go to see my mother on the way back from treatment. I feel woozy sometimes, sometimes really nauseous. Today I barf, in the wide-mouthed trashcan provided at the chapel door for that purpose.

"I know it's hard, sweetheart," she says comfortingly. "But those chemicals are going to cure you."

"They didn't cure you," I mutter. I sit down in a pew and look around the chapel to make sure I'm the only one in there. There's a light streaming through the nondenominational stained glass windows that some might find spiritual, but it just gives me an empty feeling. "I wish *he'd* been the one to go," I grouse. "You're the only thing that made our family special."

Lucy Pitkin, my beautiful mother. The banker's granddaughter. The Governor's great granddaughter, with her sheath dresses, her Virginia Woolf eyes. Lucy singing a Strauss lullaby as she tucks me in, sweeping the hair out of my eyes. Lucy perched on a stool at the diner counter, going over the books. Lucy sitting out on the front porch on a summer's evening, a highball in one hand, a collection of Sappho in the other. What she ever saw in the Neanderthal is beyond me.

"I hate the treatment center," I tell her. "It's chaos in there. So many people getting infusions, the hopped up nurses toddling around with their bags of red, blue and yellow liquid—no one's sure if we're getting the right dosage or not. Plus everyone talks the whole time, across each other, over each other, exchanging platitudes a mile a minute: Make the most of what you have; I'm not done yet; Life has to go on; Stay on the bright side—it's enough to make you want to kill yourself."

"Cut them some slack, sweetheart. They're facing their own mortality."

"You'd think it would elicit a higher level of discourse."

"That's kind of what it was like for me at the end," she says thoughtfully. "So chaotic. Everyone standing around the bed gawking—and me with my bald head at the center of it all, struggling to draw my last breath like something out of a Faulkner novel. You of all people should've known better, Spyros. I never liked those kinds of scenes."

"You're right," I say. "I'm sorry, that was horrible. We should've shot you." Her bright, trilling laugh fills the empty chapel.

"Your sister's sleeping around," she says after a moment.

"So what? Me too."

"Yes, but you know how to handle it. I don't think she's using contraception."

"Moron," I say, and then I tell her about the shoe salesman, how I keep going back to his store, his storeroom, how I can't get him out of my mind.

"Brown's Shoes? That's where we got you your first wingtips, those nice two-tones. Your father was so mad at me for buying them."

"Asshole," I say, lying down on the pew. The fatigue's kicking in.

"But he let you wear them, Spyros. Don't forget that."

She's right, I think, as I drift off to sleep. I do have a tendency to overlook my father's good deeds. The other day, I walked into the chapel and stopped short when I saw him sitting there. I'd never even entertained the possibility that he talked to her too. He nodded to me and hurried away, blowing his nose. In moments like that I think I really should cut him some slack, but then I never do.

Zoe

We've got these beautiful studios for our art students on the top floor of the hospital, but none of them wants to paint or draw or sculpt or even photograph. Especially the latter—their hatred of the photographic image is particularly intense. I think it's because we live every day under the tyranny of the all-knowing scan, those shadows and bright spots and insulting little arrows. Nobody even cares about privacy any more—people bring their scans out into the waiting room, down into the cafeteria; everyone takes a look, gives their opinion. We're very visually literate, you can say that, but we're tired of having to look.

So what does that leave? Apparently, it leaves performance art. That's all anyone in my program wants to do: performance art with a strong emphasis on vocalization. In other words, they just want to get together and scream—sometimes for thirty, forty minutes at a time. It's time-based art, I'm told. Duration is key.

And today we were given something new to scream about: the government's threatening to cut off our disability checks. They say the volume of claims they're processing is unsustainable, and they're sending out an agent to assess our situation. The insurance consortium's sending an agent out too. Dad says we should put on a show for them in the amphitheater, treat them as our benefactors—which they are in a way.

Meanwhile, I've stopped going for scans. I know there's something new growing inside me, I can feel it in my belly, it tugs and pinches, I don't need to be shown. I'm still getting treatment, I haven't given up on that, I just have no desire to see what it is.

George

My father's right. Chipeta wants nothing to do with me. Well, that's not entirely true. I think she wants a little to do with me. We're pretty much co-directing the production now—she enjoys that part, I think. Getting people to question, to speak, to move around the amphitheater.

"You're a born leader," I tell her after rehearsal one day. "You should've been a doctor."

"Is that supposed to be a compliment?"

"Do you want to have dinner with me? I could get some food from the cafeteria and we could picnic on the hillside."

She flips through her script, not even looking at me. "Picnic with a Pitkin? Never."

"Oh come on, I'm only a Pitkin on one side. And look at the mountains, they're turning blue—what a beautiful time of day for a picnic!"

"Enough with the picnic," she says, finally fixing me with a stare. "What's between you and me is no picnic." She examines me more closely. "You know you look like the Governor. That picture in the lobby."

I do look like him, which is my terrible luck, or maybe it's karma. My great great grandfather's campaign slogan was The Utes Must Go—or more precisely: the Utes Must Go on a Forced March from Colorado to Utah, Leaving Us Their Mineral-Rich Land. "But my mom was disowned by the Pitkins for marrying my father," I tell Chipeta. "Doesn't that count for something?"

"I'm sure it does with some people," she says. "You should go on a picnic with those people."

Costa

They weren't bad guys, the agents. To tell the truth, I don't know why it took them so long to get here, except for the fact that their offices were in chaos too. I spotted them sitting together in the cafeteria, two skinny bald guys in bad suits going over their notes.

I brought them a special Ute drink made from amaranth flour and honey and asked what had brought them to our fine hospital. "You don't look sick," I said, though of course they did—everyone does, except for me.

The agents smiled sourly. "Oh, we're sick alright. *We* just have to work for a living."

"Believe me, I know what that's like," I said, and they relaxed a little. They were just a couple of working stiffs.

"What's that art school over there all about?" the government agent asked suspiciously. "How come they're well enough to make art but not well enough to get a job?"

"Yeah," said the insurance agent. "They can't be as sick as they're making out."

"That's what I thought at first," I lied. "But you know, we need art in times like this. It brings order to the chaos."

The agents looked thoughtful. Maybe the amaranth drink was working on them—it was fermented. Or maybe these guys had poetry in their souls, you never know.

"They're putting on a show tonight," I said, like I didn't have anything to do with it—like I hadn't been charged with getting the two of them there. "You should come and see for yourself what it's all about."

The agents nodded, they were open to it. They already knew there was nothing else to do in this town.

Then Sanpitch came over. He was wearing a blanket, so they knew right away he was a Ute. The government stiff got nervous—they always do. I think Sanpitch put on the blanket just to get a rise out of him. "So, you come to kick them out of the hospital?" he said, by way of an opener.

The insurance agent shot his friend a look. "That remains to be seen."

"You want them to die a little quicker, huh?"

"Of course not," he huffed.

Sanpitch shrugged, adjusting the blanket on his shoulders. "Just calling it like I see it."

"What do you care, anyway?" the government agent piped up. "You Utes have been praying for them to disappear for two hundred years. Did that ghost dance and everything."

"That's what I'm trying to tell you," Sanpitch said. "Patience has its reward."

Zoe

Mom's worried about me but I don't think what I'm doing is self-destructive. Or maybe it is, but sometimes it feels good to take matters into your own hands. Like the time that gunman made his way into the hospital and went on a shooting spree. As soon as the code silver came over the intercom, everyone started running for the stairs, trying to find the shooter. When we finally located him up on the fourth floor, we rushed down the corridor in a pack, yelling, "Here we are! Come and get us!" but at the sight of so many people, he panicked and turned the gun on himself. Like all mass shooters, he was a coward. "Selfish bastard!" somebody yelled.

Yes, who's to say what's right or wrong in our situation? How about the Children's Hospital up at the top of the mountain? Is it right to have banished the children like that to languish away in the clouds? But how could we stand it otherwise? At least this way we can pretend. The nurses text down pictures of their birthday parties to their parents, and we ooh and ah, though I'm pretty sure it's always the same photo, taken from across the room.

Today Mom asked me pointblank if I'm pregnant. She said she could hear it in my voice, a certain sneakiness, like I have a secret. "I don't know," I mumble. "How should I know?"

"Take a test. Get an ultrasound."

"No more tests or scans. I'm done with all that."

"What do you mean, you're done with all that?"

"To be honest, I think there are two things in there, but only one of them's moving."

"Moving? Already? Dear God!'

"Is he there with you?"

"Not funny, Zoe. I'm trying to think. Have you been nauseous?'

"Sure, but that's nothing new."

"Okay, okay. Which feels bigger, the thing that's moving or the thing that's not moving?"

"The thing that's moving."

That seems to ease her mind a little. Honestly, I don't know where she finds the energy to care. I can barely feed myself lately, I'm so tired, and I'm not even dead.

Spyros

They were the ones who wanted to dance nude in the show—it wasn't my idea. I've given up trying to control them. There are things they want to do with their bodies, and they're just going to do them. They call it the Swirl, or sometimes the Vortex. The idea being to race round and around the stage, as fast as they can, until their bodies become a blur of flesh, and their individual sufferings melt away into something—or thingness—that's beyond ego or pain. Who am I to say it won't work?

My own impulses run in the opposite direction. Yes, we're all suffering, but we suffer in different ways and it's important to stay true to that. Plus, I actually have a little joy in my life right now—with Chris, the Brown's Shoes salesman. The way he says my name, "Spi-ros," as in spiral. Not the way my family says it. Not the way it's meant to be said. Wrong but right. The way he surrounds my lips with his, making an "o" inside a bigger "o," another spiral. It's all in the details.

My mother's worried about my sister. "Just don't let her stop treatment," she says. "Promise me that. You've got to hold out for the cure, all of you."

"Do we? Sometimes I think it would be better if we didn't. Is it really so bad where you are?"

She seems taken aback by my question. "It's not so bad," she stammers. "It's, you know, Zen, peaceful. But sort of indifferent, too. There's no love here, Spyros. No love without a body."

"But what about that transcendent, spiritual love they're always talking about? The God thing?"

"I'm just telling you how it is for me," she says sadly. "Each day a little more not-me enters into me; a little more uncaring thins the caring. And I can feel the process accelerating. I bet if you dug up my casket today, you'd see it's completely rotted away and I'm mostly bones, with just a few hunks of flesh and hair hanging—"

"Mom, stop! TMI!"

We buried my mother instead of cremating her, because according to the Greek Orthodox Church, the only way to get into heaven is in a body, and my father insisted on seeing her put in the ground. She was raised a Methodist, but she never cared about any of that stuff, she took life's experiences as they came, including death. I always thought I was like that too, but now I realize I've been cradling a mental image of her walking through the pearly gates on her own two feet, wearing the white suit and pumps we buried her in, whole and serene.

Costa

In the end, the show was everything I'd hoped it would be. I didn't think I was even going to get to see it after I got in that big fight with George. He wanted to charge admission—or in business school jargon, "to monetize the event."

"Why, in God's name?" I asked. "What are you going to do with the money?"

"Studies have shown people appreciate art more when they have to pay for it."

I didn't say anything to that, just walked over and dragged away the barrier he'd made them put in front of the entrance.

"Put it back!" he yelled. He's too weak now to move it himself.

Chipeta walked over to see what the problem was. "The barrier stays where it is," she said after I explained, and that was it, the show was free.

The agents showed up early and snagged themselves a seat in the front row. I preferred to sit high up in the back, where you could watch the performance and the Rockies at the same time. The way the light dances over the mountains in the evening, the play of blue and gold and black—I never tire of it. It reminds me of Greece. We could've been sitting in Epidauros, the ancient amphitheater in the hills.

But the agents put themselves right down in the middle of the action, which means they got the full effect of the thirty minute scream that started the show: fifty naked people, with bloated, chopped up, knobby bodies, standing there screaming with all their might. And the "dance" that followed, the silent whirring around the stage, the bodies merging into one long body, not even a body, really, more like a pouring of flesh out onto the stage and then back into the tunnel from which they'd emerged. Then it was time for questions.

Why me? Why her? Why him? Why us? Why now? Why here? Why there? Why everywhere, all over my body? How long is the treatment? How long till my scan? How long till results? How long till I die? Where are the experts? Where is the cure? Where did our tax dollars go all those years? How can this be happening to me? How can it be happening to them? How can it be happening to children? What did we do? What did we DO?

The questions rose from the stage in a big cloud of noise, but somehow you could still make them out—maybe they repeated them over and over, maybe they just articulated them nicely, I don't know. Some were sung, operatically. Others were whispered, but it was like they were whispered in your ear—the acoustics of my theater are that good.

One question persisted long after the others had fallen away. It was a man's voice, but high, strained. It was George. What is life without love? What is life without love? What is LIFE without LOVE? I was embarrassed for him, but also kind of impressed. I mean, he saw his opening and he took it.

The agents didn't move after the show. Everyone else streamed up the stairs and out of the theater, but they just stayed sitting, motionless. Uh oh, I thought, that's not a good sign. I made my way down through the crowd to where they sat staring at the empty stage.

"Gentlemen?" I said, and they turned their tear-soaked faces in my direction. The government agent broke into sobs; his buddy put an arm around his shoulders. "That was . . . magnificent!" he choked.

"You thought so?" I was genuinely surprised. "Not too . . . avant-garde?"

The government agent shrugged off the other guy's arm and sat up straight. "As long as I live," he said, his face contorted with purpose, "their disability payments will never be cut off!"

"Same here," said the insurance agent. "Same goes for their benefits!"

"That's great news," I said. "But how long are you going to live?"

The government agent slumped over. "Ten months," he mumbled. "Maybe a year."

"And me, maybe a year and a half," said the other guy.

"Well, that's something," I said, letting out my breath.

Zoe

Mom laughs when I tell her about the show, says she wishes she could've seen it. She always loved the theater, or the idea of the theater anyway—there wasn't much of it in our town. I think she would've gotten a kick out of the Institute, too; she liked it when people behaved oddly. We had a neighbor she loved to visit, a World War II vet who had served in Japan. He cut down the legs on all his furniture after he came back, so his whole house was low to the ground. I always thought that was weird, but she said it was clever.

When I tell her what the agents said, she sighs with relief. "Maybe that's enough time."

"For what? The baby or the cure?"

"Both. Certainly the baby, if there's a baby."

"Look at me, Mom. There's a baby."

"Sweetheart," she says sadly, "I can't actually see you. "

That makes me panic a little. My mother has always been able to see me. Her eyes on my face have anchored my being. Now we have only words, plus her voice is growing thin and her attention wanders. "Mom," I urge. "Tell me something about being pregnant, about birth, about being a mother."

"Okay. Well, pregnancy is the weirdest thing that will ever happen to you, except maybe cancer. To be at once a person and a container for another person is existentially quite challenging. Don't be surprised if it feels like you're hallucinating for nine and a half months. As for the birth, watch animal videos."

"Wait, what?'

"In the weeks leading up to the birth, watch videos of animals having their babies. They just get it done. And hum through your contractions. You'll be fine. No, the thing nobody ever tells you about is post-partum. That's the hard part."

"What's that?"

"It's the period after the baby's born—technically. But it takes a long time for you actually to become two separate people. You have to heal. The baby has to nurse. . . It feels like it's taking forever to get out of this world, but it takes longer than you think to get in."

"Anything else? Anything I should know about being a mother?"

"Hm? Oh, yes, know this: First your child will love you, delight in you, live for you. But after ten years she will tire of you, resent you, feel trapped by her residual dependence on you. That will go on for ten more years and then she will love you again. Then you will die."

"Aw, Mom. Don't give me a hard time. Because pregnant. Because cancer."

"Okay, never mind."

"Is it crazy to be having a baby in the state I'm in? In the state everybody's in?"

"It's always crazy, sweetheart. No sane person would ever have a baby."

I try to ask her more questions, but she doesn't respond. Lately that's been happening more and more. No one knows how much longer she's going to be here, including her. She drifts in and out of our conversations now, the way she did when I was a little girl and she was reading a book. I used to love the way her eyes soft-focused on me when I finally got her attention, as if I were a rose that had fallen into the stream of her thought, a sweet little surprise.

Spyros

Naturally, my mother's the first one to hear about my scan results. I run to the chapel to tell her.

"Darling!" she rasps.

"But I told the doctors not to say anything to anyone."

"Why?"

"I'm afraid someone will kill me. Out of jealousy, or despair. Or that people will just be really mean."

"No, Spyros," she says. "They'll worship you. They'll throng around you, wanting to know how you did it!"

"Well, I don't want that either."

'How *did* you do it?'

"I didn't do anything. I mean, I did the same stuff as everybody else, it just worked."

I've heard stories about the other epidemic, the one that started among young men like me, the one nobody cared about except those who had the disease and those that loved them. How lonely it was, compared to this one. This time we're all in it together, people like to say, as it's some great step forward for humanity that everyone's dying of cancer. But I have to admit, it does provide some comfort. Who am I to mess with that?

"You're evidence of a cure," my mother insists. "The others need to know, they need hope."

"The doctors tell us not to think in terms of cure anymore," I chide her. "They say we're almost to the point where cancer can be treated as a chronic disease. That's the goal now, to get to the point where we're living with it, not dying from it. Like AIDS."

My mother snorts, loudly. I don't think I've ever heard her snort before. "What kind of a goal is that?"

I actually think my brother and sister already know. They walked in on me in the dance studio the other night, rehearsing the male variation from Sleeping Beauty, knee-deep in virtuosity. I haven't danced ballet in years, but this is a pet project, a way of seeing what my body can do. I was going to stop when I saw them, but somehow I couldn't, my body couldn't, it was too strong, too powerful, too eager, so on I went, circling the stage, each leap and turn wholly articulated, completely controlled and yet boundless. They watched till the end without saying a word, and then, before I'd even toweled off, started in on some Institute business they wanted to discuss. But as we talked, their eyes kept scanning my body in a slightly accusatory way, as if searching for evidence of betrayal. Yes, they knew, even if they didn't yet know, and so did I.

George

I finally went to see her. I didn't know if she would speak to me the way she had to the others, I'm not spiritual or sensitive—that stuff is lost on me. But I wanted to try because I felt bad about not coming into her room when she lay dying. It was such a circus in there, everyone jostling to get to her bedside, grabbing at her hands, gabbling at her like she could still hear them. But they were right, I guess. People don't end just like that.

She spoke to me as soon as I entered the chapel and sat down. The voice was faint, hard to make out, but it was hers. "How's Chipeta?"

"You know about Chipeta?"

"Your sister told me."

"Well, she kissed me after the show—a real kiss, on the lips—but now she won't even talk to me."

"Chipeta kissed you?"

"Why do you sound so surprised?" Of course, I'd been surprised too, so surprised I barely managed to wrap an arm around her before she pulled away.

"From what Zoe said, I thought it was a one-sided thing."

"Screw Zoe. She kissed me. But she's a Ute, and me being a Pitkin—for her, that's a big problem."

"Technically, you're not a Pitkin."

"Doesn't seem to matter."

"Well, she has a point, George. The Governor killed a lot of Utes."

"I love this woman, Mom."

"That's not always enough."

"But we're artists! We're supposed to make it new!"

"Not so easy, is it?"

"And the kiss? Where does that leave me?"

She sighed. "It leaves you with a sliver of hope."

"That's it? That's all?"

"Sweetheart," she said faintly. "I'm awfully tired."

"Forgive me!" I blurted. "I really came here today to apologize for not saying goodbye to you when you were . . . I didn't know it was going to—"

"Take so long? Me neither. Well, you're saying goodbye now."

"I am?"

"I'm not exactly sure, the timing's tricky, but why don't you say it just in case?"

"Goodbye, Mom. I—"

"Goodbye, George."

When we were little, my mother always used to say she could hear things in our voices—guilt, hunger, exhaustion, even the onset of the flu. Well, I could hear something in her voice now, brightening the edges of it: laughter. I don't think she was laughing at me, per se, I think she was laughing at the whole thing. I think she was laughing because she was done.

Zoe

My daughter Lucy sits on her diapered behind, waving a dry paintbrush over a blank canvas, copying the grownups seated around her. Yes, they're painting again, and sculpting—even taking photographs. Like me, they've decided they'll have no more scans.

We're smaller in number now—some have died, others have simply left the Institute, saying it's too crazy here, too intense, that they just want to be quiet, to clear their minds before the end. We wish them well. We're here because we need to be, because our minds won't clear, because we can't be quiet. Of the Utes, only Chipeta and a few others remain, and because Chipeta's still here, George is too. Meanwhile, Sanpitch and a large contingent have moved into town. They've brought the square and the storefronts back to life. They're getting on with it.

My father and Spyros, both healthy, have formed an uneasy alliance. They're working on a new dance stage for the Institute. Spyros is relentless, the flooring must be perfect: sprung hardwood, not too slippery, not too sticky, not too hard, not too springy, not too light, not too dark, not too noisy, not too quiet—you get the picture. There have been many re-dos; I'm sure there will be many more. Dad enjoys it. Spyros divides his time between yelling at my father and sitting by Chris's bedside. It's the happiest I've seen him.

I'm weaker since the birth, tired all the time—but somehow more alive. I'd like to ask my mother if this is how it was for her, maybe this is how it is for everyone, but our conversations have stopped. She's finally fallen to the other side, I guess, if there is another side—or perhaps it's we who have fallen to this side. Whichever the case, the clasp is broken, and we cleave to other things. I keep my Lucy close; I'll never send her up to the Children's Hospital, no matter what. And there must be others who think like me at the Institute, because there are more kids around these days, running bare-kneed through the grounds.

Do we still hold out hope for a cure? Of course—don't you? It's a worthy goal. But so is a picnic. So is a kiss. So is the perfect dance floor. So is a photo of this exact moment. So is the end of a story.

The Tragedy of Ayapaneco

The Professor Has Been Called In

The Professor has been called in. There have been some complaints about her class, the Dean's email says, and he would like to discuss them.

In fact, there has been only one complaint. A student is angry with the Professor for pushing the Homosexual Agenda. "I assume you know the assignment in question," the Dean says, but the Professor is stumped. Though she is, in fact, a lesbian, she has not made any homosexual assignments in her Intro to Linguistics class.

"Perhaps if I knew which student made the complaint. . .?" she says, wracking her brain, but from the Dean's expression she can tell this is a wrong move. "Or what week the assignment was due?" she adds meekly.

The Dean clicks through his emails. "Week 6," he says tersely.

Week six, week six. "Ah!" the Professor says. "Homonyms!"
The Dean raises his eyebrows.

"Dam/damn! Whole/hole!" she sputters.

The Dean looks slightly offended. The Professor laughs shrilly. "Words that sound the same but have different meanings and sometimes spellings," she explains.

The Dean finally smiles, a small one. "I see," he says quietly, swiveling his chair around to gaze out the window at a leafy oak tree, the students crisscrossing the quad. "Well. Perhaps worth revisiting that assignment, no?"

The Professor, also smiling, is caught off-guard. She isn't sure how to revisit the assignment, nor why. The Dean doesn't swivel back around to explain.

Khalil Gets a Phone Call

Khalil gets a phone call from Florida at 6:25 am. It's a loan officer laboring under a misunderstanding. He thinks Khalil has to start paying back the interest on his student loan right away. Though he isn't really awake yet, Khalil does his best to clear things up. The financial aid officer at the University has told him he doesn't have to pay back his loans until he finishes college. The loan officer listens patiently, then says, well, this one is a bank loan, the interest must be paid back right away. It suddenly dawns on Khalil that he may be the one laboring under a misunderstanding. He feels nauseous, begins to sweat, then hangs up on the loan officer before it can be determined, once and for all, which of them is laboring under the misunderstanding.

The Homonym Thing

The Professor is having a chat with her Chair. The Chair rolls her eyes when she hears what the Dean said. "What's the University coming to?" she moans.

The Chair has a lot of strong feelings about what the University's coming to; she voices them frequently on social media. But this chat is not really about that. This chat is about the fact that enrollment is low, and the Professor, who's been teaching Intro to Linguistics on a semester-by-semester contract for the past ten years, may not be asked back next term. "And to be perfectly honest," the Chair says sorrowfully, "the homonym thing isn't going to help you."

The Professor asks the Chair when she will know if the Professor will get another contract. "We're feeling the squeeze, too, you know," the Chair deflects. By "we" she means the department's tenured professors. "They want us to start teaching the intro classes." She looks at the Professor wonderingly. "Intro to Linguistics? Where do you even begin?"

False Friend

Khalil gets another phone call from Florida, and makes the mistake of answering the phone without looking. He thinks it's a friend calling back; he was just talking to him. It's not his friend, though the loan officer addresses him casually. "Hey Khalil, what's up?" They return to their previous conversation. Khalil sighs, gives in. He has a new understanding of his loan situation: it's bad. "But how am I supposed to start paying the interest while I'm in school?" he says. "I'm already working thirty-five hours a week."

The loan officer says he wants to talk to Khalil like a human being. He reminds him that his name is Donald. "Can you just forget for a sec that I'm a loan officer?" Donald implores. "Is it okay for me to talk to you like a human being?"

Khalil doesn't say anything. Donald waits patiently.

"Yeah," Khalil says finally.

Donald clears his throat. "Well, I have a friend who got into a similar situation, and he didn't think he had any other options besides defaulting on his loan. But then he heard about plasma donation. By donating plasma just two times a week, he could afford to pay off the interest while he was in school."

Khalil wonders what the word "human being" means to Donald. Perhaps it's a false friend, he thinks (he's a linguistics major). A false friend is a word that looks or sounds the same in two different languages, but actually has a different meaning.

The Professor Has Another Job

In addition to the two courses she currently teaches at the University, the Professor has another job teaching online composition at a for-profit college. These courses pay a fraction of what she makes at the University, but she's able to conduct them year round, at night and on the weekends. In fact, she must conduct them continuously. If she fails to respond to student posts within a 24-hour period, she gets a call from the Course Advisor saying she has missed the Engagement Benchmark. If she fails to call back the Course Advisor, she gets a call from the Semester Moderator.

There's a whole team dedicated to making sure she gets back online to answer her students' questions, but when she does, she must draw her answers from a list of pre-selected phrases. The Professor has actually received retraining for answering her students' questions in her own words. She thought that would show she was going the extra mile in her online teaching, but apparently not. Sometimes she wonders why the Course Advisor and the Semester Moderator don't just enter in the pre-selected phrases themselves, instead of tracking her down.

Khalil Has Stopped Answering Phone Calls

from Florida.

An Infelicity

While pasting in pre-selected answers to her online students, the Professor puts her smart phone on speaker and listens to her voicemails. This is how she comes to hear her father's voice, his slow cruel drawl. He's out of work again, he's supporting her sister and her baby now, they need her to wire them money. "I know you've got it," he says. "Call me back, *professor.*"

In the first blush of her last significant relationship, the Professor finally came out to her family. "Affirm who you are," urged her girlfriend at the time. "Come out and say, yes, I am a lesbian. Then they can't hold it over you anymore."

But her family just saw this as putting on airs. "Oh, so now you're a *lesbian* professor?" her father scoffed.

"I am a lesbian" is a performative utterance, linguistically speaking, both a declaration and an act, but in her case, it didn't work. When a performative utterance is made under inappropriate conditions, and fails to produce the effect that it names, it's called an "infelicity."

Another Infelicity

One Sunday night, a campus security officer stops Khalil on his way to the laundry room. "I'm a student," he tells the officer, but the officer ignores him.

"What's in the bag?" he says, and Khalil swings his sack of dirty laundry off his shoulder to show him the contents. The officer springs back and puts his hand on his holster.

"It's dirty laundry," Khalil says, hurriedly opening the bag. The officer edges closer and pokes around in the laundry with his flashlight. Then he asks to see Khalil's swipe card ID.

"Okay, buddy, you're good to go," he says, barely giving it a glance. "You understand there's been some thefts from the dorms, so we're being extra careful."

The officer gets in his car and drives away. During the time he was being extra careful with Khalil, several white kids with laundry bags passed them by and now the machines are all taken.

Back in his dorm room, Khalil sits on the couch with his old friend, the bag of dirty laundry. He tries calling his mom, but she doesn't answer so he leaves a message. When the phone rings, it's Donald.

Schadenfreude

The Professor runs into the Chair in the hallway. The Chair's face is pink, and her short blonde hair is mussed. She's just come from a meeting where the Dean announced the Linguistics Department is being dissolved.

"Dissolved?" the Professor echoes. "Why?"

"Not enough majors. We'll just be offering classes for the General Ed requirements now." The Chair sighs, then brightens. "But some of us may get joint appointments in other programs—I, for instance, can teach German language classes."

So now the Chair will be teaching the intro linguistics classes the Professor used to teach, plus German. That doesn't sound all that much better than online composition, the Professor thinks, feeling a bit of *schadenfreude*.

The Tragedy of Ayapaneco

But the Professor feels no *schadenfreude* when she breaks the news to Khalil in their independent study. As an adjunct, the Professor isn't paid for doing independent studies, but it's one way to get to see her students develop.

Khalil loves to think about language. She could tell this already in Intro to Linguistics, where his questions were never about processing the lecture but always about teasing out its applications. She tells him what's happening to the department and that it means he will have to switch majors, which will set him back in his progress toward the degree. She encourages him to see an academic advisor. He says he will and then asks her, why do languages die?

They talk for an hour about why languages die. About urbanization and the state and what linguists refer to as the Tragedy of Ayapaneco. The Tragedy of Ayapaneco, the Professor explains, is that the survival of the Ayapaneco language relies on two old men, Manuel Segovia and Isidro Velazquez, who live half a mile apart in southeastern Mexico but refuse to speak to each other. They're in fine health; it's their language that's fading away. "So there's a will to language," Khalil says, and the Professor smiles.

As he's leaving her office, Khalil stops and turns around. "I have to find a new major, but we can still do these independent studies, right?" he asks. The Professor's cheeks burn as she tells him she won't be coming back next semester. And here he thought she was a real professor, delivering a real education.

The College is Being Shut Down

The Professor is furiously grading essays from her online college students when she receives a call from the Semester Moderator. "I'm grading papers," she blurts. "I'll be back online in half an hour."

But the Semester Moderator isn't calling about the Engagement Benchmark. Perhaps the Professor has already heard: the college is under federal investigation, and there's a possibility it will be shut down. The legal situation is tricky, and she's under no circumstances to say anything to her students. Class discussion boards will be monitored for inappropriate comments.

"When will you know for certain?" The Professor asks.

The Semester Moderator is more upfront with the Professor than the Linguistics Chair was. She's a businesswoman, after all. "Between you and me," she says, "It's pretty much a done deal."

The Professor gets off the phone and goes back to grading essays. At the bottom of each one, she writes: *This is your last assignment. The college is being shut down.*

Go Big or Go Home

Khalil's on the phone with Donald, talking about what his new major should be. Donald's pretty sure it should be business or computer science. "Something that will make you money after you graduate," he says. "Especially now that you're adding on the extra time."

"I was thinking philosophy," Khalil says.

Donald chuckles. "In for a penny, in for a pound, eh?"

"Go big or go home."

But Donald grows serious. "Really, now, Khalil. You have to think about your mom."

"My mom?"

"Your mom, your co-signer! Did you forget about her?"

On a Terrace in Ayapa

The Professor has a new job: Development Associate for the University. She no longer writes or teaches, and spends most of her day on fundraising calls, but she has healthcare for the first time in her life. Her office is not far from the Dean's, and as she stares out her window she can see a few branches of that same leafy oak tree, the outer edge of the quad. Half a mile away, on the south campus, Khalil sits at a monitor in Intro to Programming, learning how to code. It's not too bad—it's easy really. It's just another language after all.

Two thousand more miles away, Manuel Segovia and Isidro Velasquez share a cup of chamomile tea on a terrace in Ayapa and good-naturedly argue the finer points of their mother tongue. What nonsense, the so-called Tragedy of Ayapaneco!

Rosie the Ruminant

I like to stand at the top of the hill in the early morning, gazing down on the bright green valley wreathed in mist, the sheep clustered close to the barn like a ragged cloud. They lie down after we're let out and continue sleeping, but I breathe in the fresh, grassy air and kick up my heels—literally, I, too, am a sheep—enjoying my freedom and the feel of the wind in my fleece.

This is just one instance of my iconoclastic temperament, which I've always suspected was the reason they chose my DNA for Dolly's genetic blueprint—it's an indicator of great intelligence. Wilmut, the head scientist here at the Roslin Institute, is himself an iconoclast, a free thinker, and I feel a kinship there. For one thing, he knows that not all sheep are idiots—most, but not all. Another thing he knows, which you may not, is sheep are matriarchal. Oh, perhaps not originally, but certainly nowadays. The ram only comes around so often, you know, and for a very specific purpose. And being matriarchal, of course we'd have an interest in that final frontier: parthenogenesis.

Once the others had been chosen—Alice for her egg, Belinda for her womb—we talked it out amongst ourselves.

"Aye, right!" Belinda said skeptically. "Well, I'll be the real mother."

"Depends on how you look at it," I said. "Her genes will be mine—all of them. She'll look exactly like me, though environment will play a role in the development of her personality."

"Let's hope so, ya scunner," Belinda muttered. She and I have our differences, especially when it comes to parenting. She bonds easily with her lambs, worrying about their milk intake and sleep habits and marveling over their satiny pink ears, whereas I don't find my lambs all that interesting until they've learned to talk, by which time they're usually removed from my care and swallowed up by the flock.

"What about me?" Alice piped up, wagging her fluffy white tail. "I'm just the egg stuff?"

"Your egg will have its nucleus deleted," I explained, "and replaced with mine. But your mitochondria will continue to provide her cells with energy."

"Huh. Hey, look who's here!" She'd spotted Sire and raced off to join him. They've put on his leather apron so he can't mate with any of us right now, but that's no deterrent for Alice.

"I don't know about all this," said Belinda, watching the two of them nuzzle. "Sire's not got much going on upstairs, but I think I'd miss his company."

"No one's talking about getting rid of Sire. But aren't you the least bit tired of birthing his stupid babies?"

"He's got a good heart."

"Look at all of these dumb, good-hearted sheep," I said, swinging my head around to indicate the flock. "With no say over what we do or what's done to us."

"Oh, and she's going to change all that, your little clone?"

I did think my clone had the potential to lead our flock out of bondage. One sheep of prodigious intellect—well, I'm just a freak of nature. But two of us, and perhaps more to come—it could be the start of a revolution. "We'll name her Hippolyta," I said dreamily. "After the queen of the Amazons."

"Aye, right," Belinda said, tossing her head in annoyance. "Hippo for short."

But of course, we didn't get to name her. It was our "caretaker" old Roddy who did, just as he does all of us, silly names like Belinda and Alice and Rosie. Rosie! That's me. But this miracle, this beacon of hope for our species, he named, Dolly. Suggested it to Wilmut for the coarsest of reasons, that they name her for a human singer with large teats since they sucked my DNA out of a mammary gland cell. And Wilmut, nodding and laughing and snorting away, communing with Roddy on the crudest level—oh, that was a low point! Does he know what his shepherd does after hours, how Roddy takes his pleasure with the ewes, all but me and a few others who stamp down hard on his execrable toes?

Dolly's birth, five short months later, was amazing. All births are: that one life comes from another, that everything starts all over again, that we are given yet another chance. But Dolly's birth was doubly amazing, because she was my exact clone, so it was *I* who was being given another chance. After the joyful news came, and all the rumors that she would have two heads or six legs had been put to rest, I went off to the top of the hill to ruminate. Being a ruminant and having to chew your cud several times a day provides ample time for reflection, if you're not always worrying over your lambs, or flitting off after some ram in an apron. I looked down at the lab and the barn and wondered who amongst us had brought this creature into being, us with our bodies or them with their pipettes and petri dishes, their electric spark?

Belinda's quite convinced it's us—or her, rather—they'll never replace the womb, she says. But maybe they'll decide they have to someday, if we cease to offer it up so willingly and actually demand something in return. The human females have already struck their deal; they have their marriages—though if Mrs. Roddy's condition is any indication, it was a fool's bargain. It's she who does most of the work around the barn, dragging pails of feed from stall to stall on old Roddy's orders. "There, no, not there, there, ya eejit!" he calls from the doorway as she scuttles back and forth, their fifth bairn trailing miserably behind her. If that's what a wedding gets you, I'll take my chances.

The day Belinda and Dolly were released from the lamb jug and I laid eyes on my clone for the first time had to be the best day of my life. I say had to be, because while I possess a far superior intellect to most sheep, my long-term memory is more typical of the species. To tell the truth, I've stretched it a bit even to get this far with my story.

Broad-backed Belinda came out first, heavy and tired but smiling beatifically; then Dolly gamboling along behind her on long, skinny legs, wagging her fluffy white tail. I inspected her from a short distance: she seemed perfect in every way. Of course, upon rumination, I understood that she appeared perfect because she was a miniature version of me. She was a perfect *copy*. Same white face, horizontal ears and white fetlocks—but not merely similar in color, the exact same. So much so that the other ewes kept swinging their heads back and forth between us, as if their world had rotated on its axis.

"Handsome is as handsome does," I chastised them. What I was dying to know was if she was curious, if she was bright—had she inherited my powers of observation and critique? Would we be able to join forces and lift our flock out of the muck of ignorance and apathy, into the light of freedom?

I made my way through the other ewes until we came face to face. I had wondered if she would run to me and nuzzle at my teats, but she merely stared at me with the same curious, open expression with which she took in the rest of the flock. Environment: 1, Heredity: 0.

"Hello, Dolly," I said. She seemed startled that I knew her name. "Has your mother told you about me?"

Dolly shook her head. Belinda was probably giving her time to bond, but I felt it important to lay out all the facts of her existence right away. I wanted her to know she wasn't like other lambs, and okay, I wanted her to know she had my DNA. With Belinda's back turned and the rest of the flock trying to horn in on the feed grain she'd received to aid with lactation, I took the opportunity to fill Dolly in on all the details. I knew she wouldn't get it—she was barely a month old—but at the very least I wanted to lodge a seed of doubt in her mind as far as Belinda was concerned. Not for spiteful reasons, mind you, but to encourage my clone to embrace and nurture her gifts as they became apparent.

I launched into what I considered to be an exceptionally clear explanation of the cloning process—clear, but not dumbed down—and Dolly listened with apparent interest. But halfway through, she abruptly walked off in search of Belinda and a snack. Was she flighty, this clone of mine?

"Is that her?" Alice asked, coming to stand beside me.

"Yes," I said proudly. "That's her."

"Funny, she doesn't look like you at all. Oooh, is that feed grain?"

And Alice was off again. Was it possible? No, I couldn't bear to think it.

I wrote off my first interaction with Dolly due to her extreme youth, but as she matured, she sadly showed no signs of turning into—well, me. I tried to connect with her several times, tried interesting her in animal husbandry, cloud formations, the constellations—anything at all. But she soon began avoiding me, running off with her little friends whenever she saw me coming.

"You should be glad she's fitting in," Belinda said. "Do you want her to be a miserable snob, like you?" Normally, Belinda's barbs don't get to me, but I must've looked a little hurt, because she added gently, "Try talking *to* her, not *at* her."

And it was true, Dolly was sweet and spirited and everybody liked her, which I guess counts as success from a cloning standpoint—after all, she could've been rejected by the flock. Instead, she'd been quickly embraced, and her unusual origins just as quickly forgotten.

"But she's not a seeker," I protested.

"Aye right, a seeker!" Belinda chuckled. "Is that what you are?"

The day Dolly turned eight months old, the lab team decided it was time to announce her existence to the world. The world of humans, that is. What a circus! For a week straight, Wilmut gave interview after interview to the hundreds of reporters trampling the pasture—all that sweet, lovely grass laid to waste—and always with Dolly standing in the background. Sometimes Belinda and I crowded into the picture (Alice couldn't care less), but he never mentioned us once.

To be honest, though she was the focus of great attention, I felt a little sorry for Dolly, having to stand there on display day after day. She seemed confused and depressed, and I only wished she'd stayed still for my explanations, so she could at least follow what Wilmut was saying about her now. And then there were the protesters who came each morning to picket the lab. The humans had been surprised, caught off balance, and some of them had turned nasty. No one had thought cloning was right around the corner, and now they were afraid one of *them* might get cloned next and sidestep the reproductive process. If that happened, they seemed to believe, cloning would catch on like wildfire, resulting in God's wrath and/or designer families incapable of unconditional love.

If only I could've been interviewed, I might have put some of their fears to rest. Oh, I can attest to the satisfaction of physical self-duplication, but it's a fleeting triumph, since it's really your soul you yearn to see recreated, to live on *as you* after you die, and that, in my experience, is just not the way it goes—with a bairn or a clone. And I could've told them there is no God, and saved them a lot of worry.

It wasn't a surprise to learn old Roddy had his own designs on Dolly. One night, not long after her unveiling, some of the ewes overheard him chatting to the missus about his dastardly plan. Mrs. Roddy tried her feeble best to dissuade him, but he brushed her objections aside. He was planning to kidnap Dolly and sell her for a high price to the wealthy American who'd just bought up Invereray Castle—wealthy Americans were always looking for conversation pieces, he said, and Dolly was certainly that. Plus, he could easily blame the kidnapping on the Christians, or the animal rights activists, or any number of the daft bampots who'd been swarming his barn of late.

Once word spread of Roddy's scheme, there was general consternation amongst the ewes that their dear Dolly might be taken from them. I myself felt somewhat ambivalent at the prospect. What new and life-changing experiences might she have, there on the estate of the wealthy American? What intellectual horizons might open up to her? At the very least, to what historically and architecturally significant buildings might she be exposed?

"For chrissake, ya numpty, it's not like she's going away to boarding school!" Belinda snapped. "You'd really let old Roddy make off with her?"

"Well, what do you expect me to do?" I mumbled.

"She's your *clone*. If you'd wash that manky face of yours, you could pass for her in her stall, if the night was dark enough and he didn't see the heft of you."

"And what? Get myself kidnapped instead?"

"Oh, come on then. You can handle Roddy."

And handle him I did, with a swift kick to the groin, and one more to the head for good measure. There was a moment where I considered turning my back on the flock forever and venturing forth into the world as Dolly's replacement, but I knew my subterfuge wouldn't survive the dawn. And to be honest, I was interested in seeing our little experiment through.

Roddy lied to Wilmut about what happened—no surprise there, either. He said it was the animal rights activists who'd clobbered him as he wrested Dolly from their self-righteous hands, knowing the scientist would be inclined to believe him. Wilmut hated the animal rights people; they got to him in a way the Christians didn't. And

Mrs. Roddy backed him up with her "eyewitness account," and that was that. From then on, Dolly was locked away each night in the lab for her own protection, and old Roddy kept his distance. At first, the other ewes bleated her name through the night, but after a while, you know—the long-term memory thing.

And I don't think it's actually an unhealthy arrangement. Having some alone time every evening, that headspace to herself, has made Dolly more thoughtful and introspective. She comes looking for me now, and tells me that she wants to learn. She remains a difficult pupil—in science and math she's nearly hopeless, but unlike myself she's shown a real aptitude for poetry. Predictably, her verse is chock full of pastoral imagery—green hills and grey rocks, misty mornings and all that—but I have to say, it sings. She rushes to share her poems with me as soon as she's released from quarantine, and then, when I encourage her, with the rest of the flock, her devoted fans. When Dolly's up on a rock reciting her newest verses, nothing can tear the other ewes away, not even the rattle of feed grain in the trough.

My Dolly's become a leader, I guess, though not in the way I'd foreseen. She didn't lead us out of servitude, but she's nurtured our love of freedom and creativity, and that, I think, has strengthened the flock and made us all more reflective—attuned to the extraordinary in the ordinary. Even I see revolutionary possibilities now where before I saw none—in Belinda's infinite capacity for love, for instance, and Alice's headlong pursuit of pleasure. We haven't figured it all out yet—how to live with no gods, no shepherds, in control of our bodies and our reproductive destinies. But we know what the important questions are, and we're ruminating on them.

NOVELLA

The First Daughter Finds Her Way

The First Daughter Finds Her Way

1

Wendy scrambled up the stairs of the secret passageway and slammed the Solarium door behind her, her ragged breath echoing through the bright, quiet room. She'd just been cornered by a tour in the corridor between the Red Room and the Blue Room, thirty or forty people rushing forward like a wave, upending her body in a roiling breaker of arms and legs until the Secret Service appeared to put a stop to it. "What are you doing down here?" the agents yelled at her. "Get back up to the quarters!"

She'd only been trying to slip out into the Rose Garden for a breather, but she'd mistimed her mad dash. Those self-guided White House tours were difficult to avoid. Visitors were always wandering off the designated pathways—peering up the stairwell into the First Family's living quarters, sitting at the Green Room writing desk or racing their hot wheels across the Entrance Hall's parquet floor. The American People were a capricious people, she was beginning to suspect, or at least they seemed to have a little trouble with impulse control—especially when it came to her, the First Daughter.

The First Daughter. It sounded like such a simple, elemental thing to be, but it was actually quite complicated and confusing. Were they rushing forward because they loved her or because they hated her, or was it simply the madness of crowds acted out on a lonely emissary of power? Once she'd overheard one of the guards telling a story about Andrew Jackson, how an admirer sent Jackson a huge cheddar cheese weighing fourteen hundred pounds, and how he invited the American People into his home to eat it, which they did in a matter of hours, grinding the crumbs into the carpets with their muddy boots, so that for months afterwards the White House stank of cheddar. *So he thinks he's the Big Cheese*, she imagined them saying. *Think again, Andy.*

Plus, she was only fifteen, a teenager already struggling with the great mad crowd inside of her, the bilious stew of competing identifications churning in the pit of her stomach. Wendy crossed over to the Solarium's long bank of windows and pressed her forehead to one, allowing herself to drift—the cool glass against her brow a little spot of calm in the maelstrom, a wormhole to an easier time.

Because she hadn't always lived in the White House. Once upon a time, she'd lived in a house like any other, a house behind a hedge. To be honest, she didn't remember much about the house behind the hedge, except that the living there was easy. She liked to run around the yard in the noonday sun like a crazed rabbit, happy and floppy, or hoppy and flappy—whatever, it was fun. In the evenings she lay quietly on her back in the blue-green grass and sang to the first stars. The stars circled in one direction and her head in the other, and in between them, twisting, was the sky.

Life was simpler for her parents then, too, in the house behind the hedge. Her father was an attorney and her mother was an attorney's wife. Politics was a distant horizon, a hazy possibility they sat in front of at the end of the day, chatting in low, interested voices. They were both ambitious, in their different ways, but their ambitions hadn't yet taken anything from them or anyone else, their ambitions were good—to do good. Wendy had no idea what they were talking about over there on the Adirondack chairs, but neither did they really.

In those days, no one noticed that her hair grew in tufts, or that she had sweaty palms, and they hadn't yet caught on that one of her eyes was lazy. Her parents even played games with her. One day her mother chased her around the garden, shrieking "ticky ticky ticky," until Wendy fell into the rosebushes and crushed them. Another time, her father came home from work and stood watching her flop around in a flowerbed with a faint smile on his lips. His briefcase had a shiny metal edge that reflected the dying sunlight into her eyes, blinding her. "My father is God!" she shouted at the top of her lungs, burying her face in the dirt. It was only a game, but it made him uncomfortable and he went inside.

It wasn't until he decided to run for Governor that anyone took a really good look at Wendy.

"Oh darling, your eye!" her mother gasped. "How long has it been like that?"

Her father frowned. "What are those bald patches in your hair?"

"Can she even hear us? Do you think she's gone deaf?"

And so Wendy got an eye patch in short order, and a shampoo that burned her scalp, and was told not to look away when people spoke to her, but to nod at them and smile, even if she wasn't interested in what they had to say. When she said, "What's the big deal? Nobody cares what I do," her mother pursed her lips and sat her down for a little talk about Representation. Representation was her father's job, and her mother's job, and now it was her job too.

"People look to you for inspiration, darling," her mother said. "They look to you to be something they can't."

"Why can't they?"

"Because you're the One who Represents the Many."

"Why can't the Many Represent the Many?"

"Because there are too many Many."

Wendy thought it over. "Is that why we ride in parades?"

She hated riding in parades, sitting between her mother and father in the apple red convertible. How they perched on the trunk with their feet on the back seat and turned and waved and smiled. How little girls glowered at her from the sidewalk and sometimes stuck out their tongues. Turn wave smile wave turn smile smile. How you could never tell what the crowd was going to do when you passed by, and how they waited until the last possible moment to do it. Smile turn wave smile wave turn smile. When they clapped, it was such a relief. Usually they were clapping for the marching band coming around the corner, but who cared? At least they weren't jeering. Turn smile smile turn wave smile wave.

If only we could be the Many, and not the Ones! Wendy sighed, because deep down, she loved parades. She loved how the paraders lined up on those leafy side streets out of sight of the spectators, and how restless and excited everyone got waiting to move. She loved it when the long line of convertibles, floats and marchers turned that first corner, and the show was on. She loved it when the first half of the parade went too fast and the second half too slow and the crowd started to think the show was over. But no, look! It's the Shriners, closing the gap in their little toy cars!

If I were the Many and not the One, Wendy thought, then I could just sit and watch the parade like everybody else. She pictured herself with a balloon in one hand and a hotdog in the other. Kicking back in a pint-sized folding chair, with zinc on her nose. And she pictured another little girl stopping in front of her in an apple red convertible, a balding little girl with a lazy eye nobody really wanted to look at. Who knows, she might even feel sorry for that other little girl, and jump up to offer her the balloon, and the other girl might reach down to take it. But then the convertible would lurch forward and the other girl would lurch backwards and move on, and Wendy would sit back down with her balloon to wait for the marching band coming round the corner.

Now those dreams would never come true. Now that they were the First Family, representing the entire country, their every move was scrutinized and would be to the end of their days. Consider what happened during her father's inauguration in January. It started out perfectly fine: the swearing-in on the Capitol steps went off without a hitch, and the parade afterwards was spectacular, with a hundred marching bands and a thousand floats and a hundred thousand red, white and blue balloons. The mood was heady and hopeful, and at a certain point the new First Family threw caution to the wind and got out of the limo to walk the parade route—a decision they instantly regretted, it was so cold. Their eyes streamed tears as they waved their frozen hands: turn smile smile turn wave smile wave. The American People waved back cheerfully—they were wearing mittens, and had portable heaters blasting under their chairs.

Later that evening, the President and the First Lady waltzed together onstage in a packed ballroom while everybody watched: her father's back ramrod straight and his chin held high, her mother's head thrown back and her eyes half-closed. They looked like they were on top of the world, which they kind of were. But then the First Lady's eyes fell upon Wendy and opened slightly in surprise. The next time she whirled by, her eyes opened even wider, and the third time they nearly popped out of her head. Because somehow, somewhere, Wendy had managed to change out of her Inaugural ball gown and into a bright orange jumpsuit. The First Lady murmured something to the President and they rushed over and bundled her into her coat, hustling her out the side door in a matter of minutes, but it was too late, the American People had already seen.

And what they had seen had upset them. Was it a prank? A statement? A fashion statement? Why orange? Why orange? Did the new First Daughter think they would fall for any old color, just because she was wearing it? Certainly she didn't expect her bright orange *schmatta* to go on view in the Smithsonian Collection with all of the other First Daughters' dresses from inaugurations past! But were they to include in the collection the dress she *should've* worn, the heartbreakingly beautiful designer ball gown her mother had picked out for her—in a patriotic shade of blue and beaded all over like a million tiny tear drops—that wouldn't be strictly factual. Maybe if the placard were changed to "beaded dress to have been worn by," or "intended for," or "designed for"? But then museumgoers might think the dress had failed—that the First Daughter had chosen another, better dress not currently on display—when in truth it was the First Daughter who'd failed.

Did they really care that much? Oh yes they really did, or the Press said they did, and what other way was there to know? According to Randy, her father's chief of staff, the only way for the First Family to get past it was for Wendy to go on TV and explain her choice in person.

And so, in the blink of an eye, the First Lady's style team had manicured Wendy's nails, whitened her teeth, waxed her mustache, plucked her eyebrows, shrunk her pores, blown out her hair, squeezed her into a blue dress with slimming vertical red stripes and navy pumps with three-inch heels, and slathered her with pancake makeup and mascara. She was going to be interviewed on prime time TV, because that's where all of the nation's deep emotional issues got worked out, in hour-long interviews conducted by sympathetic lady reporters named Diane and Barbara. There'd been some debate as to which one it should be, Diane or Barbara, but in the end Randy decided on Diane, because Barbara always made her guests cry. It wasn't so much that he was afraid Wendy would cry as that she wouldn't, and then the American People would never forgive her.

And so, a mere twenty-four hours after the Inauguration, Wendy followed her mother on set, clomping along behind her in her new three-inch heels. Peering through her lacquered lashes, she shook hands with Diane, who reacted to her clammy palms with only the slightest twitch of the lips—a mark of true professionalism, since right then Wendy's hands were the clammiest they'd ever been. Her mother thanked Diane for the opportunity to set things straight and went and stood behind the cameras, and Diane and Wendy sat down in mauve armchairs in front of a fake fireplace. Somebody yelled out "five-four-three-two-one!" and Diane turned to her with a blinding smile.

"Okay, let's start with the obvious question. Why orange?"

Wendy shifted uncomfortably in her chair. "Why not orange?"

"Ha ha ha. No, seriously. Why orange?"

"I like orange?"

"You like orange."

"Yes."

Diane narrowed her eyes. "You wore orange to the Inaugural Ball because you like orange."

Wendy nodded.

"Now we're getting somewhere. Why do you like orange?"

"Uh—because it's orange?"

"You like orange because it's orange. Do you like any other colors?"

"Yes."

"Like red? Or white? Blue?"

"Sure."

"Why didn't you wear one of those colors then?"

"A lot of other people were already wearing them."

"So the orange was a statement? And the jumpsuit?"

"Well, jumpsuits are very comfortable. And I was planning to dance."

Diane re-crossed her legs impatiently. "Some people think you were trying to communicate your feelings about moving into the White House—or perhaps taking a stand against mass incarceration. Because you know, prisoners wear orange jumpsuits."

Wendy smiled wanly. "I didn't know that."

Diane sat back, regrouping. "Tell me, who did your hair today, Wendy? It looks very nice."

"Uh—the hair man?"

"And your dress is by?"

"I don't know."

"Well, did you pick it out yourself? It's very pretty."

"My mother picked it out for me," Wendy said hesitantly, sensing another trap, "but I said okay."

"Okay?"

"Yes."

"Just okay?"

Wendy looked wildly around the studio for a way out. She couldn't see past the cameras, though, because of the lights.

"What are you thinking about right now, Wendy?" Diane asked, as the camera zoomed in on her guest.

"Um—the end?"

"The end of what?"

"The end of this whole thing."

"Do you mean Armageddon?" Diane asked excitedly.

Wendy covered her face with her hands. "Can we please stop?"

And that's when the First Lady stepped in. Diane had to pretend to be glad to see her and cut to commercial while they pulled up another chair, but she was secretly fuming because she'd been on the verge of a revelation—right at the lip of it, or in the lap of it, whatever—and that's what drives up ratings for a lady reporter. But now it was all about the First Lady's lemon cookie recipe and a new look for the State Dining Room, and the First Daughter had gotten away.

Though not entirely. The next day the wires sent out a still from the show and all of the papers ran it—some above the fold, some below, but always the same shot of Wendy peering out at the studio audience, headband askew, mascara smudged, and, it would appear, third finger lifted in the direction of the camera, though this she tearfully denied.

There was no getting around it, she was going to have to address the American People again. But this time Randy chose a different format.

"Just write an Open Letter and we'll run it in all the major newspapers."

"What's an Open Letter?"

"Open up and tell them who you are. What it's like to be you. That's all they really want to know. You're making this much harder than it has to be."

Wendy breathed a sigh of relief. She felt much more comfortable writing a letter than doing TV interviews. She quickly scribbled out a draft and handed it over.

AN OPEN LETTER TO THE AMERICAN PEOPLE
FROM THE FIRST DAUGHTER

I am often asked, what's it like, being the First Daughter? It's like being in a long hallway, a long hallway with orange at the end. You never get to the orange, though, because you are always waiting. Waiting for the thing to start. Waiting for the thing to end. Waiting for the people to arrive. Waiting for the people to leave. Waiting for the next thing to start. Waiting for more people to arrive. Waiting to arrive at more people.

It is next to. Next to and nearby and sometimes instead of. When it is instead of, it is heavy and full, when it is next to, it is light and empty. It is alongside. To the right or to the left. If it is in the center, it is really in between, except when it is instead of. It comes closest to being in the center when it is instead of. When it is not instead of, it can only be alongside. To the right or to the left. Sometimes it is behind or in front, but for all intents and purposes, it is alongside. It is only truly in the center, behind or in front when it is instead of.

It is looking. Looking and looking. Looking at people. Looking at people looking. Looking at cameras looking. Looking at cameras looking at people. Looking at cameras looking at people looking at cameras. Looking at cameras looking at people looking at cameras looking at people. Looking at people looking at cameras looking at people looking at cameras. It is touching. Touching and touching. Touching hands. Touching shoulders and upper arms. Never touching breasts or legs. It is feeling. Feeling and feeling. Feeling hands. Feeling shoulders and upper arms. Never feeling breasts or legs. It is smiling. Smiling and smiling, down the long hallway, smiling at the orange at the end.

Love,

Wendy

"Are you nuts?" snapped Randy, when he had read it through. "We can't print that!" Instead, he drafted a different Open Letter for Wendy to sign. This was common practice in the White House, her mother explained, even for the President. Especially for the President, who had so many demands on his time.

AN OPEN LETTER TO THE AMERICAN PEOPLE
FROM THE FIRST DAUGHTER
(revised)

Dear American People,
I'm having so much fun in the White House! There's a basketball court here, and a tennis court and a swimming pool and even a bowling alley!! There are secret passageways, too, like the one behind the door in the wall outside the Queen's Bedroom that goes up to the third floor Solarium, where you can see the Washington Monument!!! And a movie theater, where you can see movies before they're ever released!!!! Thank you for electing my dad President!!!!! You're the best!!!!!!

Hugs & Kisses,

Wendy

The revised Open Letter ran in all the major newspapers, and the scandal quickly blew over. The American People came to see the new President's Daughter as just a normal, excitable teenage girl, albeit a bit challenged in the looks and fashion departments, and the Press turned its attention to more important matters, like celebrity pregnancies and basketball. From Wendy's perspective, the only good thing to come out of the whole ordeal was discovering the secret passageway up to the Solarium, her new favorite spot in the White House. No one else was ever there, except her mother sometimes to water the plants, and there was indeed a magnificent view of the Washington Monument.

2

"Wendy? Everything okay?"

Wendy lifted her forehead off the glass. Her father was standing in the Solarium doorway.

"The Prime Minister of Japan is here for dinner," he said. "Why aren't you dressed?"

"I am dressed."

"Dressed for dinner. You're wearing a sweat suit."

She pointed out the window at the Washington Monument. "Look!"

"Don't change the subject. Not many girls get to meet the Prime Minister of Japan, you know."

"I know," Wendy said, her voice catching. A single tear wound its way down her nose and dangled from the tip.

The President stepped forward, then back, then forward. "Honey?" he murmured, patting the hood of her sweatshirt. "Is something wrong?"

She wiped her nose on her sleeve. "Dad, what am I doing here?"

"I was wondering that same thing."

"Not here in the Solarium. Here in the White House."

The President sighed. "We're here to serve the American People, honey."

"But the American People hate me."

"That's not true. You two just got off on the wrong foot."

She started to sob and the President looked around the Solarium in a panic. "Where's your mother?"

"Probably being styled," Wendy moaned. "She's always being styled!"

"Listen," the President said, casting about for something comforting to say. "Listen to me. You can make a difference!"

She stopped crying abruptly. "I can?" she whispered.

"Yes—um—you could take on a cause!"

"A cause?"

"Sure, the White House takes on causes all the time! But this—this could just be yours."

Wendy's eyes lit up. "I could have my very own cause?"

The President smiled. Crisis averted. "Absolutely. We've got to go down to dinner now, honey, but give it some thought."

The very next morning, Wendy went to see her father in the Oval Office. "Daddy," she announced proudly. "I've found my cause."

"Your what?" the President muttered, without looking up from his newspaper.

Wendy paused, feeling dizzy, as if the Oval Office were spinning around her. She always felt that way in the Oval Office, because it had no corners. "Remember last night when you said I could have my own cause?"

"Oh, right," the President said, folding the newspaper and motioning for her to sit down in one of the yellow armchairs across from his desk. The Oval Office was mostly yellow, but unlike the Green Room, the Red Room, the Blue Room and the White House, it was defined by its shape, like the Pentagon. When does shape trump color? she wondered, momentarily distracted.

"And your cause is?" he prompted her.

"What? Oh, yes. Pain."

"Pain?"

"Yes, I would like to call people's attention to the fact that there's too much pain in the world."

"The American People?"

"Well, yes."

"American pain?"

"No, not just American pain."

The President looked thoughtful. "Okay, but you've got to narrow it down. How about crippled children?"

"Crippled children?"

"Honey, if you're going to take on a cause, you need to stay focused, which is not to say you can't be creative. How about landmines?" The President snapped his fingers. "Children crippled by landmines!"

Wendy smiled politely. "I'd rather stick with too much pain in the world, but I see your point. Let me try breaking it down." She took a piece of paper from the presidential notepad and wrote furiously while he talked on the phone. When he was done with the call, she read her list out loud:

the pain of abandonment

the pain of acceleration

the pain of adaptation

the pain of aging

the pain of aha!

the pain of AIDS

the pain of alarm

the pain of anachronism

the pain of apartheid

the pain of arbitration

the pain of assassination

the pain of atavism

the pain of auction

the pain of avalanche

the pain of awe

the pain of babble

the pain of beauty

the pain of bias

the pain of blackness

the pain of boredom

the pain of breach

the pain of bulimia

the pain of cancer

the pain of celebrity

the pain of chador

the pain of circumcision

the pain of clairvoyance

the pain of cohabitation

the pain of crack

the pain of Cubism

the pain of—

"Enough!" the President interrupted, holding up his hand. He was going to tell her to forget it, the words were right on the tip of his tongue, but to his surprise, he felt a burst of father love. Father love is when you love something, not because it's deserving, but because it's yours.

"You may be on to something there, honey," he said instead. "Keep going and we'll see."

Perhaps we should explore what else the President is thinking about at this time. Get inside his head and find out what, or if, he's plotting. Because whatever the President of the United States is plotting is going to affect a lot of people, not least of them his daughter.

It turns out the President's main preoccupation at the moment, fittingly enough, is the American People. Some days he thinks he knows what they want, and other days he's totally mystified, not unlike Wendy. It only really matters when he has to make a decision of some sort, and then he asks his advisors, well, how do the American People line up on this issue, and they conduct a poll. The truth is, the American People don't seem to be all that interested in what he's doing, so it's just a matter of checking in with them now and then to make sure that they don't mind. He only ever proposes the tiniest little initiatives, anyway, which are largely designed to appeal to their self-interest. And if for some reason they do seem to mind, his advisors tweak the wording of the question and do the poll over, which usually works out fine.

When he isn't thinking about the American People, the President spends a lot of his time thinking about previous American presidents, and comparing himself to them. He knows there's no way he'll ever be able to compete with his predecessors on the level of deeds, since in his era historic events are few and far between, and largely generated by the media. There's no real way he can compete with them on the level of words, either, since in politics words acquire weight from deeds, otherwise coming across as so much hot air. No, the only thing this President really has going for him are his looks, but there he thinks he actually has a pretty fair advantage. Pundits have called him "the most Presidential-looking President since Kennedy," which is a balm to him and also a reminder to keep up appearances.

Sometimes, when he's trying to get his head around his presidency, he pictures the United States as a nation of sleepwalkers, and sees his job as protecting the American Dream. To keep the American People from waking, he hums the same lullabies their parents' presidents hummed to them. When they stir, he whispers "U-S-A!" or "no new taxes!" and sends them back to sleep with smiles on their faces. And if they happen to catch a glimpse of him before drifting off again, he assures them by his grooming and demeanor that the nation is in capable hands.

Today, after Wendy leaves, he gets right back to work—which is to say, he goes right back to inspecting photos of Kennedy taken in the Oval Office. He compares Kennedy's Oval Office to his—there's the same white marble mantel, the same presidential seal on the ceiling and the two flags behind the desk, and although those aren't Kennedy's crossed swords hanging on the wall, the President has put up a pair of his own, a gift from the Naval Academy. His desk is different, too, but his chair is an exact replica of the one Kennedy's personal physician designed to ease his chronic back pain. The President doesn't have chronic back pain, but he thinks that might well be because he has Kennedy's chair.

Most of all, the President looks for similarities between Kennedy's expressions and his own, because if he can't be a president who matters, he can at least look like one who did. There's that famous photograph of Kennedy sitting at his desk in the Oval Office on the phone that the President thinks of every time he's sitting at his desk in the Oval Office on the phone. Kennedy's covering his left eye with his left hand and the President would give anything to know why—in shock at what he's hearing? Or is he simply feeling the weight of the world?

And how about that other famous photo of Jack with his little son and daughter—the shot of the two children dancing around the Oval Office while Jack watches them from a straight back wooden chair next to his desk? His heels are raised, as if he's jiggling his knees up and down in time to the music, and just in front of the children you can see a line of adult-sized footprints in the deep blue pile of the Oval Office carpet. This particular photograph gnaws at the current president because there's no way of recreating that scene, not merely because he's the father of an awkward teenage daughter rather than two angelic toddlers, but because those are the heavy steps of History outlined there in the carpet—Khrushchev's? Johnson's? King's?—and those feet don't pass through the Oval Office anymore.

So at this moment, the President isn't plotting. At this moment, the President is listening to the gentle snores of the American People, and mingling his sweet breath with theirs.

"The pain of Darfur!" Wendy shouted, when she burst in on him a few hours later. "The pain of D.D.T. The pain of death. The pain of digression. The pain of docibility. The pain of drag. The pain of duplication. The pain of editing. The pain of effigy. The pain of egad! The pain of ejaculation. The pain of elegance. The pain of emancipation. The pain of ephemera. The pain of equivalence. The pain of error. The pain of escape. The pain of ethics. The pain of evolution. The pain of execution. The pain of fat. The pain of fear. The pain of fiction. The pain of flopping. The pain of forgetfulness. The pain of free trade. The pain of Futurism—"

"Honey?"

"The pain of gardening," she continued, ticking it off on her fingers. "The pain of genetics. The pain of ghosts. The pain of girls. The pain of governing. The pain of greatness. The pain of guests. The pain of gym. The pain of habit. The pain of hindsight. The pain of homelessness. The pain of hunger. The pain of hypochondria. The pain of icons. The pain of ideals. The pain of ignorantism. The pain of illiteracy. The pain of immigration. The pain of incest. The pain of irony. The pain of isolation—"

"Honey!" her father snapped and Wendy paused. For the first time, she noticed an enormous man with a droopy mustache and several chins, sitting like a walrus on the yellow sofa.

"This is the President of Russia," her father said, and Wendy walked over and stuck out her little fish of a hand. *"Rad znakomstvu."*

The Russian President took her hand sadly, and his mustache rose and fell. "Nobody has known more pain than the Russian People, little daughter," he said, adding thoughtfully, "except, perhaps, the Poles."

The American President smiled politely, but he was annoyed. For the last hour and a half, he'd been hearing about nothing but Russia's pain. The rampant inflation, the alcoholism, the organized crime. What did you expect? he felt like saying. You lost the Cold War.

"Soooo muuuuch suuuuuffering!" the Russian President wailed. "First the Tsar and his Cossacks. Then the Revolution. Then the World Wars. Four million dead in one winter! Then Stalin. And now, capitalism!"

"But can't you do anything about it?" Wendy asked. "As President?"

The Russian President sighed, taking a Cuban cigar from the American President's secret stash and lighting up. "That is why I'm here, little daughter, but your father doesn't seem to care about pain."

Wendy turned to her father. "But the pain of jazz, Daddy! The pain of Jewishness. The pain of jibberish. The pain of jokes. The pain of judgment. The pain of kamikazes. The pain of keening. The pain of kindergarten. The pain of kleptocracy. The pain of knowing. The pain of kooties. The pain of Kurds. The pain of labor. The pain of leaving. The pain of liquidation. The pain of losing. The pain of lunchtime. The pain of lymphoma."

"Yes, yes," the Russian President said, reaching for yet another cigar and ferreting it away in his inside coat pocket. "And how about this for pain? No longer being able to afford even one lousy box of Cohibas!"

Wendy nodded eagerly and the two of them entered into a call and response routine as her father looked on helplessly.

W: The pain of memory—

RP: A once great nation torn to pieces!

W: The pain of migrants—

RP: Those wretched capitalist dupes!

W: The pain of motherhood—

RP: Russia, your children have deserted you!

W: The pain of mutation—

RP: And the horror of irredentism!

W: The pain of myopia—

RP: Why didn't we see this coming?

W: The pain of narrative—

RP: Why must it end this way?

And so they went, on and on through the pain of negation, the pain of niceness, the pain of nothingness, the pain of nuclear proliferation, the pain of nympholepsy, the pain of obduracy, the pain of occupancy, the pain of oddlings, the pain of ogling, the pain of Ohio, the pain of old age, the pain of omission, the pain of opposition, the pain of ordinariness, the pain of osteoporosis, the pain of otherness, the pain of outsiders, the pain of overexposure, the pain of owing, the pain of pacifism, the pain of pedagogy, the pain of piffle, the pain of poverty, the pain of prison, the pain of psychoanalysis, the pain of publicity, the pain of queens, the pain of quitting, the pain of rape, the pain of realization and the pain of righteousness, until finally the President grew so alarmed by his rapidly depleting cigar stash that he pretended to be late for a meeting with the Chinese ambassador and hustled them both out the door.

The Russian President looked out over the garden and inhaled deeply. "The pain of roses!" he sighed, and bowing to the First Daughter, waddled away down the colonnade.

"The pain of Russia," Wendy muttered to herself as she stumbled through the garden.

"What?" said the First Lady, who was there inspecting the gorgeous red American Beauty she'd been keeping her eye on. It wasn't actually the gorgeous red American Beauty she'd been keeping her eye on, that one had been picked weeks ago, but she hadn't been down to the Rose Garden in a while.

Every now and then, in a rare free moment, the First Lady liked to stroll through the Rose Garden in a green straw hat, carrying a basket on her arm and a pair of shears. Here and there she stopped to gaze upon a rose, pinching the stem between her thumb and forefinger. Sometimes she bent over and sniffed, and then she either snipped it or she didn't. When she had a dozen roses in her basket, she handed it over to the Head Gardener. The ones she'd picked were then arranged in a vase and placed in a faraway corner of the White House where nobody ever went, because the gardeners had already gathered up all of the really good roses at dawn.

Wendy drew up short when she saw her mother and kicked at the ground.

"What are you doing, darling? Don't tear up the grass."

"Um, well, I asked Daddy if I could take on the cause of World Pain and he said I could but I'd have to break it down. So I'm walking through the Rose Garden trying to break it down."

"World Pain?" echoed her mother. "What on earth do you mean?"

"I mean there's too much pain in the world."

"And what do you propose to do about it?"

"I thought I could just start by calling attention to it."

The First Lady looked skeptical, but told her to go on.

"The pain of sacrifice. The pain of scandal. The pain of sex. The pain of shabbiness. The pain of simulation. The pain of skepticism. The pain of slander. The pain of small towns. The pain of snubs. The pain of sorrow. The pain of speech. The pain of squatting. The pain of staring. The pain of suburbia. The pain of swallowing. The pain of tachycardia. The pain of testimony. The pain of theory. The pain of titles. The pain of torture. The pain of tradition. The pain of turntails. The pain of twins. The pain of tyrants—"

"Oh how tedious!" the First Lady interrupted, turning back to her roses. "Nobody wants to think about all of that. You're better off leaving the causes to your father and me."

"But—"

"For instance," her mother said, turning back around, "one of my causes is muscular dystrophy. We can't cure it yet, but one day we'll be able to—it's a realizable goal. The pain of tradition, on the other hand, is not curable. The pain of small towns—I don't even know what you're talking about there. Well, maybe I do, but that's just how it is."

Wendy sat down on a bench. She suddenly felt very tired. It's no easy task, breaking down the pain of the world.

"What are you doing now?" the First Lady asked suspiciously.

"Pausing," she answered, looking up at the patch of sky over the White House. It was blue and clear, a no-fly zone.

When she stepped back into the Oval Office, her father was on the phone with his stylist, scrutinizing a photo in his hand.

"No, no, it needs to be shorter on the sides," he was saying. "Longer on top."

"The pain of udders," she started up as soon as he was done. "The pain of Uganda. The pain of ulcers. The pain of umbrage. The pain of uncertainty. The pain of upset. The pain of urbanism. The pain of usury. The pain of utilitarianism. The pain of uxoriousness. The pain of vaccination. The pain of vengeance. The pain of vice. The pain of volunteers. The pain of vulgarity. The pain of waking. The pain of weddings. The pain of wisdom. The pain of women. The pain of yearning. The pain of yielding. The pain of youth. The pain of yuppies. The pain of zeal. The pain of zits. The pain of zoos. The pain of zygotes." She took a deep breath and exhaled. "There, I've broken it down for you. I mean, it's only the tip of the iceberg, but I think I've shown the way. Now will you let me present my cause to the American People?"

The President smiled tightly. He was impressed, and honestly a little flummoxed. He hadn't expected such tenacity, let alone alphabetizing skills, from his daughter. "I, um, well, that's great, honey, but you know, Randy's going to have something to say about this. It's a little . . . off-message."

"Dad," Wendy said, looking him in the eye. "Come on. You're the *President*. You don't have to listen to Randy."

The President smiled again, a looser smile. She's right, he thought to himself. I am the President. And shouldn't the President be able to give his daughter what she wants?

As predicted, Randy was livid when he heard the news. "Is this really how you want to go down in the history books?" he yelled at the President. "As a bleeding heart loser? And an indulgent father to boot?"

But the President, being President, prevailed.

The first thing Wendy did in her presidentially sanctioned campaign to raise awareness of World Pain was to seek authorization for a new national K-5 curriculum from the Congressional Committee on Education and the Workforce. The units were as follows:

The Pain of Being Born

The Pain of Being a Child

The Pain of Being an Adult

The Pain of Realizing One's Own Limitations

The Pain of Realizing the Limitations of Others

The Pain of Unemployment

The Pain of Employment

The Pain of Unrequited Love

The Pain of Requited Love

The Pain of Aging and Disease

The Pain of Death

The Committee on Education and the Workforce was appalled. "What do you expect us to do about all of that?"

At the moment, Wendy explained, she wasn't asking them to do anything, she just wanted to raise people's awareness. "And your committee could lead the way," she suggested brightly.

The Committee's raucous laughter pealed through the marble halls of the congressional office building and tinkled out onto the sidewalk, prompting giggles from passersby. What were their elected officials up to in there? After what seemed like an eternity, the Chair wiped his eyes and poured himself a glass of water. "You really expect us to tell our constituents their children need to learn about pain?"

"That would be wonderful, Mr. Chair."

Mr. Chair smirked, hamming it up for C-span. "Don't you think they know enough about it already? According to this curriculum, life is one long agony!"

The committee erupted in laughter again. An ancient grasshopper of a congressman, hailing from one of the furthest, driest western states, raised his bony hand. "Mr. Chair, can I ask a question?"

Mr. Chair nodded and sat back in his chair, still chuckling.

"Young lady," rasped the congressman. "What about freedom?"

"Freedom?"

"Our God-given right *not* to think about other people's pain—our right to look after our own damn interests!"

"Oh. Isn't that called selfishness?"

"No, it's called freedom, and it's a lot easier to legislate than compassion."

Wendy fiddled with her papers and took a deep breath. "Well, Congressmen, I guess I'm asking you not to take the easy way out this time."

The Committee members placed their hands over their microphones and conferred.

BANG went the Chair's gavel. "Request denied!"

Since she couldn't even get her curriculum out of committee, Wendy decided to bypass Congress altogether and take her case straight to late night TV. Late night TV was where all of the nation's domestic and foreign policy issues got addressed, in conversation with funny talk show hosts named Jay and Dave. Randy was dead set against the idea, of course, but again, the President prevailed.

"So tell me, what good does it do us to be aware of pain if we can't do anything about it?" Jay asked her, stroking his smooth-shaven chin.

"Well, we certainly can't do anything about it if we're not aware of it," Wendy answered, smiling out at the studio audience. The studio audience stared back at her sullenly.

"And how exactly do you plan to increase our awareness?"

"It has to start early, before kids learn to harden their hearts. I prepared a national K-5 curriculum with that in mind, but the Committee on Education and the Workforce voted it down. So now I'm thinking, just as there's a Presidential Fitness Medal, there could also be a Presidential Medal for Awareness of Pain."

"The pain of pushups," Jay said, mock-seriously. The studio audience howled with laughter.

"For some people, yes," Wendy responded, but no one could hear her over the din.

Dave took a different approach. "Why so glum, kid? Lighten up! You've got snipers on your roof! How cool is that?"

Wendy shook her head earnestly. "What would be cool is if we all joined together and—" But she never got to finish her sentence. WAWA! came a sob over the sound system, and Dave and his studio audience began to laugh. WAWAWA! went the noise machine and they laughed and kept laughing—heads thrown back, hands in the air—all the way through to commercial.

The phone rang in the Oval Office. The President picked up.

"Are you watching this?" Randy said.

"Yes."

"And are you going to tell her to drop it now?"

"Yes," the President whispered, raising his left hand to cover his left eye.

3

As skeptical as she'd been of Wendy's campaign to raise awareness of
World Pain, and as much as she wanted to say I told you so, the First
Lady restrained herself, because she knew her daughter was hurting
inside. She felt her pain, the way mothers do. They can't help it—their
children were once connected to them, and those nerve endings never
dull, which is why mothers seem so scattered and crazy most of the
time. Our society isn't really set up for that level of involvement. The
President on the other hand, while proud of Wendy for giving it her
all, had moved on. Set his sights on other things, the way fathers have
to—or get to, anyway.

And so it was the First Lady who came to the bedroom where her
daughter lay in the middle of the day with the green velvet curtains
closed.

"Darling?" she called out.

No reply.

"Darling, you have to get up now."

"Why?" came the muffled response.

The First Lady tried to think of a reason. "Because you have to
go to school."

"It's summer vacation," said a small voice, clearer now, as if a pillow
had been removed from a face.

"Oh. Well, you can't just lie there."

"Why not?"

The First Lady tried again. "Because you're the president's daughter."

"I'll just stay here till it's over."

"Till what's over?"

"The presidency."

Though politically speaking, the First Lady thought that might not be such a bad idea, her maternal instincts told her it was. "Why don't you go for a walk in the Rose Garden, get some fresh air?"

"I'm sick of the Rose Garden."

"How about a movie in the movie theater then?"

"I'm sick of the movie theater. I'm always the only one in there."

Well if you didn't insist on watching those dreadful Werner Herzog films, your father and I might join you sometime, the First Lady wanted to say—but again, she held her tongue. "Would you like to have a birthday party?"

"My birthday's in March."

"I know, I know," the First Lady said, making a mental note of it.

"March fifteenth."

"Yes, of course, darling, but nobody else has to know that. We could do it next week. We could invite the Daughters of Congress."

"The Daughters of Congress?"

"Why yes!" the First Lady said, suddenly taken with the idea. "The House AND the Senate! That's upwards of five hundred girls!"

"Ugh." Wendy said, pulling the pillow back over her head.

The First Lady marched over to the bedroom window and drew the curtains. "What's it going to take to get you out of that bed, young lady?"

There was a long pause while Wendy thought it over.

"Can I rivermicemouse?"

"What?"

"Can I rivermicemouse? Cheese?"

"Take that pillow away from your mouth!"

Wendy removed the pillow and sat straight up in bed, her hair crackling with static electricity.

"Can I leave the White House?"

"Leave the White House? Of course, darling! Where do you want to go? We'll make a day of it!"

"The Library of Congress," Wendy whispered, her bottom lip trembling. "And I don't want you to come."

The First Lady's nerve endings responded before she did, and a terrible shiver ran through her body. "Why not? I'm your mother!"

"Yes, but you're so famous, you'll cause a big commotion. Plus you'd be bored there. You're not allowed to talk."

When the First Lady reported their conversation to the President, he had a nice long laugh.

"Keep on laughing, buddy, and you'll be sleeping in the Lincoln Bedroom."

"Relax, honey! She can't get into any trouble at the Library of Congress."

Of course that was easy for him to say, since none of his nerve endings were exposed, but the First Lady reluctantly gave her permission and Wendy got out of bed for the first time in weeks. She was going to have to take her Secret Service detail with her, but she was used to that. The agents would sit behind her in the great circular reading room and make farting noises out of the corners of their mouths, the way they always did whenever she took them somewhere quiet and dull. And when she got up to request a book at the circulation desk, one of them would stage whisper to the others, "Windy's on the move!" ("Windy" being her lazily conceived Secret Service code name) and swoop down the aisle after her in his long black trench coat. Having thus secured the attention of the entire Reading Room, he would proceed to talk to his buddies through the microphone in his lapel the whole time she was occupied with her transaction—reporting back on the name of the library clerk, the name and call number of the book Wendy had requested, the amount of time the request was supposed to take and so on. And the poor clerk would stammer and hiccup at this naked display of power, and Wendy would look up at the beautiful lady on the Reading Room dome, who personified Human Understanding, and try not to feel ashamed.

Same thing when she stepped out into the hall to stretch her legs— except then all four agents would tag along behind her, flapping in and out of marble alcoves as she wandered around looking at all the statues of famous male philosophers, scientists and artists that lined the library walls. And if she somehow managed to duck into the Members of Congress Room without their noticing and closed the door behind her, it would be:

SS1: Windy AWOL! Windy AWOL!

SS2: Isaac Newton negative?

SS1: Isaac Newton negative!

SS2: Socrates negative?

SS3: Socrates negative!

SS2: Christ!

SS1: Where's Christ?

SS2: No, I mean, Jesus, we're screwed!

SS3: I don't see Jesus! Where's the Jesus statue?

SS2: Forget it! Try Beethoven!

SS4: Beethoven negative! Negative!

But at least there, hidden away in the Members of Congress Room, a small, beautifully appointed reading room reserved for the elected officials who sadly never came to the Library (a shrine, really, to Jefferson's idea that they would come), she'd be able to sit in peace for a few minutes, looking up at the seven ceiling panels collectively titled the Spectrum of Light, each panel a different color and featuring a different beautiful pale-skinned lady representing some aspect of the Enlightenment: the indigo Light of Science, the blue Light of Truth, the green Light of Research, the red Light of Poetry, the violet Light of State, and last but by no means least, the orange Light of Excellence.

"I'd like to understand the American People," Wendy said to the

Reading Room clerk. "Could you recommend some reading?"

"She'd like to understand the American People," her bodyguard stage-whispered into his lapel. "She wants some reading recommendations."

The clerk raised a shaking finger and pointed to the exit. "Try the American F-f-folklife Center, Mr. Alan Lomax. Down three f-f-floors and to your r-r-right."

"Proceeding to the American Folklife Center," her tail relayed, close on her heels. "Somebody get a line on this Lomax character."

Situated far away from the pomp and circumstance of the Main Reading Room, the American Folklife Center was housed in a small dusty room at the end of a long blank hallway. Wendy begged her bodyguards to just case the joint and then remain outside at the entrance, as they sometimes did when she went into a confined space. After a brief huddle, they agreed, and then descended upon the unsuspecting American Folklife clerks, turning over their waste paper baskets and poking through their trash, as she looked on helplessly.

"What the hell's going on here?"

Wendy turned around to find a tall, stooped man with a shaggy white beard standing in the doorway. "Who are you?" she asked.

"Who am I? Who am *I*? I'm Alan Lomax, the Librarian of American Folklife!" he snapped, drawing up to his full height. "Who are *you*? Never mind, I know who you are. Let me pass!"

Wendy quickly stepped aside, because there are few things in this world as fearsome as a Library of Congress librarian. They have right on their side, as all librarians do, but they also have might, which is not as common. In a matter of minutes, her Secret Service detail had been eighty-sixed from the American Folklife Center.

Once her bodyguards were stationed outside in the hallway, Lomax relaxed and turned his attention back to Wendy. "Okay sister, what's your story?"

Now it was her turn to stutter. "I-I-I—"

Lomax mopped his forehead with a handkerchief, waiting.

"I w-w-want to understand the American People!" she spat out finally. "I just can't seem to reach them."

A smile spread over the old man's face and he stuffed his hanky into the pocket of his dusty suit jacket. "Well, alrighty then!" he said, clapping her on the shoulder. "You've come to the right place, m'dear. Everything you need to know about the American People—or the soul of the American People anyway—is right here, in these books and photographs and records." He jerked his thumb toward the hulking wooden card catalog. "See for yourself."

And so, sheltered from the eagle eyes of the Secret Service, Wendy set about exploring the American Folklife Center collection. The first thing she discovered was that once upon a time, the American People had experienced a Great Depression, brought on by a stockmarket crash and widespread unemployment, plus the fact that the crop-bearing middle of the country had turned to dust. To her surprise, she learned that Congress had not laughed at this Great Depression, the way they now did at World Pain, but had instead provided shelter for the Dust Bowl refugees and put them to work clearing roads and building schools and bridges. They initiated cultural programs too, including one that involved Library of Congress staff setting up shop in migrant camps to record the old folk songs and tall tales. People who came down to the social halls and took a turn at the microphone got a record to take away with them, and the Library of Congress representatives got a record to take away with them, too, which is how the American Folklife Center came to be so full of folk expression from that time.

Wendy returned to the Center the next day and the day after that, and then every day the whole summer long, making her way through box after box of material. One afternoon, Lomax pulled out a stack of Woody Guthrie albums to play for her. "You can learn a lot about the American people from this guy," he said. "He hopped freight cars all across the Dust Bowl, making up songs about the people he met along the way." And indeed, it didn't take Wendy long to recognize what Woody was trying to do: break down the pain so that the American People could get a handle on it. His song titles were a veritable catalogue of human suffering:

California Blues
Chain Around My Leg
Dust Bowl Refugees
Dust Pneumonia Blues
Dust Storm Disaster
Going Down That Road Feeling Bad
Hard Times
I Aint Got No Home
Lonesome Valley
Lost Train Blues
Worried Man Blues

"And this is the one that should've been our national anthem," Lomax said, setting the needle down on his old-fashioned record player. Wendy remembered the tune from when she was little and started to sing along:

This land is my land
It isn't your land
You better get off, before I shoot your head off
I've got a shotgun and you ain't got one—

Lomax grabbed the needle and the song screeched to a halt. "The real words to *This Land* are the opposite of that playground ditty!" he said sternly. "This land is my land this land IS your land."

Wendy's eyes grew round. "You mean Woody Guthrie was a Communist?"

Lomax chuckled. "Not exactly—he didn't like anyone telling him what to do. But he was sympathetic to what he called the economic argument. What was it he used to say? 'I ain't necessarily a Communist, but I've always been in the red.'"

Another day, he played her a bunch of Leadbelly recordings he'd made with his father, who'd been the Librarian of American Folk Life before him. "We drove all around the Deep South one summer, recording work songs sung by black prisoners. In Angola, we met Huddie Leadbetter, and my father made a recording of the song he'd written to the governor about his case, called "Please Pardon Me." We played it for Governor Neff, and he granted him the pardon! Then after Leadbelly got out, we recorded him for the Library. Woody and Leadbelly—between the two of them they really made this country feel something."

Wendy looked thoughtful. "Mr. Lomax? Would you say at their core the American People are a feeling people or an unfeeling people?"

The old librarian scratched his beard. "You know, even after all these years, I still don't know the answer. But I think that's the question—now more than ever."

So long as *they* didn't have to listen to folk music, everyone at the White House was pleased with the Library of Congress and the distractions it afforded the First Daughter. In fact, the Secret Service grew so comfortable with the idea that they stopped policing the entrance to the American Folklife Center altogether and took up residence in the Library of Congress cafeteria instead, with periodic patrols. Some days they didn't even show up until closing time, which is how Wendy came to be walking alone down Pennsylvania Avenue on the day of the Terrible Event.

She'd been standing in line to get a muffin from the coffee cart near the library entrance when she first noticed the river of people spilling down the wide marble steps of the Capitol building. Not long after that, they began streaming out of the Supreme Court Building and the Library of Congress, too. Everyone was silent to begin with, just concentrating on getting down those slippery white steps, but when they reached the sidewalk they turned to each other and started making fearful questioning noises, which is how she came to know there had been a Terrible Event without yet knowing what it was.

Lost in the crowd, she felt frightened and strangely exhilarated. No one was paying any attention to her. When she looked up, she saw FBI agents running along the roof of the Supreme Court and fighter jets taking off from across the river. When she looked back down, everyone was walking away in different directions. She thought she should probably walk away somewhere too, but where? For the first time in her life, she wished the Secret Service were there to tell her what to do.

Eventually she decided to walk home, a straight shot down Pennsylvania Avenue through the clusters of nervous, teary people gathered outside of their office buildings and businesses. When she reached the White House, the guard waved her past his booth with a dazed expression. Everyone else was going in the opposite direction, away from the residence, and it looked like he was thinking about going that way too.

Inside the White House it was deathly quiet. "Hello? Hello?" she called out. "Where is everybody?"

She found her parents sitting downstairs in the Bunker at the War Room conference table, glued to a wall of televisions. Her father's Cabinet sat with them, plus Randy and that sweet, shy guy who was always hanging around her mother—who was he again? Oh right, the Vice President. But there were other people there she'd never seen before, many of them in military uniforms, standing against the wall with arms akimbo, as if lending structural support to the Bunker.

"I called you down hours ago!" her mother murmured, patting the seat next to her, and Wendy realized they'd all assumed she was upstairs. They'd certainly received no reports to the contrary, since her bodyguards had repaired to a Georgetown drinking establishment as soon as they discovered she was missing. When they finally stumbled into the War Room later that day, red-faced and weeping, Wendy would greet them smilingly as if nothing had happened, and after a moment of stunned silence, they'd wipe away their tears and give her the new code name Princess.

But meanwhile it was only ten thirty in the morning, and she was watching the Terrible Event unfold on many televisions at once. Of those present, Wendy and her father probably felt most responsible for what they were seeing, and they bowed their heads and closed their eyes simultaneously. They stayed that way for so long the First Lady begged the Surgeon General to check their pulses. When they finally came to, their reactions were very different, although not exactly opposite. "This is war!" the President yelled, banging his fist down on the table, at the same time Wendy groaned, "So much pain!"

The First Lady was having yet another reaction, of which she was deeply ashamed. The First Lady was silently screaming, I've got to end my affair with the Vice President before anyone finds out! Surprised? It had been a surprise to her, too. But with her daughter always away at the Library of Congress and her husband otherwise occupied, she'd lapsed, big time. So big she hadn't been able to tell her pastor about it, not even when he came to do a special prayer session with her in the Solarium. Especially not then, because that was where she went for special sessions of another kind with the Vice President.

The fact is, neither the First Lady nor the Vice President had expected to feel so— well, *secondary* once they got to the White House, and that feeling had drawn them together. Plus, the Vice President was so nice and unambitious. Oh, sure, you've got to have ambitions for a presidential candidate to even think of naming you his Number Two, but your very naming means from then on you will never be Number One. And so the First Lady and the Vice President had found themselves in the same place at the same time, though they'd travelled different roads to get there.

In this and other respects, the Vice President was a little like a woman, but the First Lady liked that about him, and what's more, he was a wonderful lover, which was not unimportant to her, since she was at the tail end of her sexual prime, which had mostly gone to waste. He had hours and hours to kill, unlike her husband, plus he could recite poetry and knew a thing or two about roses. Honestly, his favorite pastime seemed to be looking at her and listening to her talk. Lying with him on the Solarium sofa, gazing out at the Washington Monument, she often thought to herself, this is the sort of man I should've married.

But she could see that was all hogwash now. It was Judgment Day, or everyone was treating it that way, and she had better get her priorities straight. Which is why, when the Vice President reached for her in the dark hallway outside the War Room where she'd gone to pull herself together, she jumped back. Though every fiber in her body wanted to jump forward, she jumped back. And the Vice President reflected upon this and understood—because he was very attuned to her feelings—it was over between them, at least for now.

For a few weeks, the American People's own reaction to the Terrible Event appeared to oscillate between Wendy's and the President's— actually leaning more towards the former (sorrow) than the latter (bloodlust). Wendy gathered this not from news reports but from the chatter she was suddenly hearing in the air all around her, a sort of collective keening. Eulogies for the victims. Choked apologies. Sobbing. Singing. A name whispered over and over in the dead of night. Fists thumping walls. Sobbing. Silence. Eyelashes fluttering in the dark.

For the very first time, she thought she might actually be hearing the American People speak without any interference from the Press, and what they were saying surprised her. This hurts, they were saying to each another. This really hurts. It's like a sinkhole's opened up in the middle of America, and I'm scared we're all going to slide down into it. No we won't. We won't. We have each other. I'd never said a word to my neighbor in eighteen years and last night we went up on the roof and smoked a joint. He gave me a bag of lemons. Everything's different now. I'm going to be different too. I'm going to be better. I'm going to join the Peace Corps. Is there still a Peace Corps? Well, something. It was a side of the American People Wendy had never seen before, and as terrible as the circumstances were, she was glad. Because if they could finally let themselves feel their pain instead of denying it, think what a better society it would be.

But one day without warning the chatter changed, and suddenly the names she was hearing in the air were no longer those of the victims. The new names were strangely impersonal, like the names of boats or racehorses, and they were being enunciated clearly, quickly and coldly.

"Do you hear what's in the air?" she asked her father one day out of curiosity. She figured if anybody else was hearing it, it had to be him.

The President looked up wearily from his desk. "What's in the air, honey?"

"All of those weird names: Copper Green, Dark Winter, Epic Fury, Freedom Eagle, Grecian Firebolt—do you hear them?"

Her father's eyes widened. "Where did you get those?"

"I told you, they're in the air."

The President got up and came around the desk, moving carefully, as if she were a bomb or a feral cat. "Honey, I need to know where you got those names. Did you see them written down somewhere?"

But Wendy curled up in a corner of the sofa and refused to talk. If she were the only one hearing those names, then maybe she'd been the only one hearing the collective keening, and if that were true, then maybe she was crazy, and if she was crazy, it was better not to say another word.

The President called in Randy, the Joint Chiefs of Staff, the Secretary of Defense, the Director of the FBI, the Director of the CIA, the Director of the Secret Service, and as an afterthought, the Vice President, but she wouldn't tell them anything either.

"Those are classified programs she knows about," said the FBI.

"Security operations," said the Secret Service.

"Secret missions," said the CIA.

"Goddamn!" said Randy.

"Goddamn!" echoed the Joint Chiefs of Staff.

"Maybe she is just picking up chatter," the Vice President suggested, but the others ignored him.

"Honey," the President said, squatting down in front of her as if he were just any old father. "We're about to declare war in response to the Terrible Event, and we need you to tell us who leaked you the names of those covert operations."

"Who are you about to declare war on?"

"We're about to declare war on Terror."

"How can you declare war on a feeling?"

The President stood up and glared at her, then turned on his heel and went to stand at the window with his back to the Oval Office. You see, this time the President really is plotting something. He stands at the window with his back to the room because Wendy's question raises a sore subject. No one knows better than he that wars are waged on hostile nations, not feelings, but that's just not the leadership opportunity he's been afforded. He's been handed an event, that's all—a Terrible Event—which has jolted the dreamers from their slumber and given him a chance to make History.

But to make History, the President knows he has to come up with a response to the Terrible Event that's as big as the terrible feeling the event has left behind, and nothing is as big as war, he figures, except maybe not-war, but that takes a long time to understand, millennia really, and the American People are still a young people, teenagers more or less, with their love of fast cars, fast sex and fast food, and impatience with diplomacy and coalition building. But feelings they get, and feelings are forever, so a War on Terror, once started, never has to end. And if this war never has to end, then unlike FDR, that other great wartime President—the one who coined the expression "we have nothing to fear but fear itself" (and okay, he meant something different by it, but it's still a nifty phrase)—this President will be setting the world's agenda for a very long time. Yes, things are looking pretty good—for the President, at least, but he doesn't especially care to lay it all out for his daughter.

Instead of answering Wendy's question, the President turned to his advisors and said, "Maybe she is telling the truth—maybe she did just pick up some chatter. She's always been a little, you know..."

"Touched," volunteered the Secretary of Defense.

"Weird," said the CIA.

"Loopy," nodded the FBI.

"Difficult," opined the Secret Service.

"Stubborn!" sighed Randy.

"Cross-eyed?" observed the Joint Chiefs of Staff.

"*Sensitive*," hissed the President, and the meeting was over. His advisors filed sheepishly out of the room, except for the Vice President, who lingered by the sofa until her father had returned to his desk.

"I hear it, too," he whispered to Wendy. "The chatter." She nodded expectantly but the Vice President just shrugged and ran a hand through his thinning hair. "What can you do? There are secret missions going on all the time. Thousands of them."

"Without our permission?"

"Why do you think there are U.S. military bases all over the world?"

"But can't we do anything to stop them?"

The Vice President put his finger to his lips. "See you down in the Bunker," he whispered, and opened the door to the thick, sweet smell of roses.

A few days later, the President declared war on Terror at a White House press conference, and everyone moved down to the Bunker for good. In single file, they carried down their mattresses, sleeping bags, footie pajamas, eye pillows, aromatherapy machines—the works. They were in it for the long haul. The Generals unbuttoned their collars, the White House staff un-tucked their shirttails, and everyone kicked off their shoes except for the First Lady, who was a lot taller in heels. Then they sat around an increasingly fetid and litter-strewn War Room watching the news and taking turns imagining when and where the next Terrible Event would occur, until by the end of each day they were so worked up no one could sleep, which meant most of the important decisions in the War on Terror were made in the wee hours of the morning.

The decision to bomb Harare, for instance—Zimbabwe's capital city—was made at three am, thanks to the burst of energy and giddy hijinks produced by a well-timed pizza delivery. The President just had a hunch—and the CIA thought it plausible—that the Zimbabwean government might be harboring the men responsible for the Terrible Event.

"But what about all of the people in Zimbabwe who aren't responsible for the Terrible Event?" Wendy asked when she discovered the plan the next morning. "Won't they get bombed too?"

Nobody heard her question, or if they did they ignored it, because it was time to get her dad cleaned up for the press conference. Randy and the First Lady did what they could, but the President wasn't so easy to clean up these days. Now that he was making history, he no longer cared about appearances—or hygiene, for that matter. He didn't care if his hair was greasy and his eyes had big circles under them and his suit—the same suit, he'd been wearing it for weeks—was rumpled and dirty, with sweat stains under the arms. Wendy watched him shamble out of the Bunker door, wiping his palms on his pants and muttering. If he was going to take up a cause, she thought sadly, why did it have to be this one?

That night and the next day and the night after that, they watched the bombing of Harare on the War Room TVs—all of those little white lights exploding. The Generals provided running commentary and hot wings were delivered to the Bunker several times. Everyone sat around licking red sauce from their fingers and periodically congratulating the President on a job well done.

And then there was the hollow-eyed man chewing nicotine gum who'd appeared that night out of nowhere to take his place at the President's right hand. Nobody knew who he was, and the President never bothered to introduce him. When Randy finally worked up the courage to ask the stranger himself, he replied tersely, "Just an interested businessman." But the Interested Businessman went everywhere with the President, bedded down next to him on the Bunker floor, and whispered in his ear throughout War Room conferences. Some said he got the contract to rebuild Harare before Harare was ever bombed.

In the thirty-sixth hour of the bombing, Wendy tried to stop it. She stood in front of the wall of televisions, waving her arms to get her father's attention, and yelled, "Hey, Dad! Dad! Do you really think the American People are going to support this? And what about all of the other peoples in the world? Don't you care what they think? What about the Afghanis? The Albanians? The Algerians? The Andorrans? The Angolans? The Anguillans? The Antiguans? The Argentinians? The Armenians? The Arubans? The Australians? The Austrians? The Azerbaijanis? The Bahrainis? The Bangladeshis? The Barbadians? The Belarusians? The Belgians? The Belizians? The Beninese? The Bermudans? The Bhutanese? The Bolivians? The Bosnians or Herzegovinians? The Brazilians? The British Virgin Islanders? The British? Well, I guess they're happy to go along. But the Bruneians, what do they think? The Bulgarians? The Burkinese? The Burundians? The Cambodians? The Cameroonians? The Canadians? The Cape Verdeans? The Caymanians? The Central Africans? The Chadians? The Chileans? How about the Chinese? The Chinese Macanese? The Colombians? The Comorians? The Congolese? The Cook Islanders? The Costa Ricans? The Croatians? The Cubans? The Cypriots? The Dominicans? The Dutch? The Ecuadorians? The Egyptians? The Emirians? The Equatorial Guineans? The Eritreans? The Estonians?

The Ethiopians? The Faeroese? The Falkland Islanders? The Fijians? The Filipinos? The Finns? The French Guianese? The French Polynesians? The French? The Gabonese? The Gambians? The Georgians? The Germans? The Ghanalans? The Gibraltarians? The Greeks? The Greenlanders? The Grenadians? The Guadeloupians? The Guamanians? The Guatemalans? The Guineans? The Guyanese? The Haitians? The Hondurans? The Hungarians? The Icelanders? The Indians? The Indonesians? The Iranians? The Iraqis? The Italians? The Ivoirians? The Jamaicans? the Japanese? The Jordanians? The Kazakhs? The Kenyans? The Kiribatians? The Kittsians or Nevisians? The Koreans? The Kuwaitis? The Kyrgyzs? The Laotians? The Latvians? The Lebanese? The Liberians? The Libyans? The Liechtensteiners? The Lithuanians? The Luxembourgers? The Macedonians? The Madagascans or Malagasy? The Malawians? The Malaysians? The Maldivians? The Malians? The Maltese? The Marshall Islanders? The Martinicans? The Mauritanians? The Mexicans? The MicDonesians? The Moldovans? The Monacan or Monegasques? The Mongolians? The Moroccans? The Basotho? The Mozambicans? The Myanmarese? The Namibians? The Nauruans? The Nepalis? The New Caledonians? The New Zealanders? The Nicaraguans? The Nigerians? The Niueans? The Norfolk Islanders? The Northern Mariana Islanders? The Norwegians? The Omanis? The Pakistanis? The Palauans? The Palestinians? The Panamanians? The Papuans? The Paraguayans? The Peruvians? The Pitcairn Islanders? The Poles? The Portuguese? The Puerto Ricans? The Qataris? The Reunionese? The Romanians? The Russians? The Rwandans? The Sahrawis? The Saint Helenians? The Saint Lucians? The Saint Vincentians, Vincentians or Grenadines? The Saint-Pierrais or Miquelonnais? The Salvadoreans? The Sammarines? The Samoans? The Sao Tomeans or Principeans? The Saudis? The Scots? The Senegalese? The Serbs? The Seychellois? The Sierra Leonians? The Singaporeans? The Slovaks? The Slovenes? The Solomon Islanders? The Somalis? The South Africans? The Spaniards? The Sri Lankans? The Sudanese? The Surinamese? The Swazis? The Swedes? The Swiss? The Syrians? The Tadjiks? The Taiwanese? The Tanzanians? The Thais?

The Tibetans? The Timorese? The Togolese? The Tokelauans? The Tongans? The Trinidadians and Tobagans? The Tswanas? The Tunisians? The Turks? The Turkomans? The Tuvaluans? The Ugandans? The Ukrainians? The Uruguayans? The Uzbeks? The Vanuatuans? The Venezuelans? The Vietnamese? The Virgin Islanders? The Wallis and Futuna Islanders? The Welsh? The Yemenis? The Zambians? The Zimbabweans? What must the Zimbabweans be thinking right now, with their capital city in flames?"

The room fell silent and all eyes turned to her father, who raised his hand in seeming benediction. But no, he was motioning his daughter away from the TVs. When Wendy failed to respond, he turned to her mother, and the First Lady grabbed her by the elbow and dragged her from the room.

"Just what were you trying to pull in there, young lady?" she snapped when they got out into the hallway.

"What do you mean, what was I trying to pull?" Wendy said, twisting out of her grasp. "What's he trying to pull?"

"What were all those made-up countries you were yelling about?"

"Those weren't made up! Those are all of the other countries in the world!"

"Oh," her mother said, patting her hair back into place. "Well, nobody likes a showoff."

"I wasn't showing off," she said miserably. "I was trying to get Dad to see that the American People are just one people among many others."

"Yes, of course," the First Lady said impatiently, inspecting a hot sauce stain on her sleeve. "He knows that. But there's only a group of eight or so that really matter. And within that group, we matter most."

"So that means no one can stop him?"

"I'm afraid not, darling. The United States is a Superpower. The only remaining Superpower in the world." Her mother smiled sadly, whether at the state of the world or the hot sauce stain, Wendy couldn't be sure.

"But if we're a Superpower, then why do we need to bomb other countries?"

The First Lady looked thoughtful. "I guess your father wants to send a message. In case people are beginning to think we aren't so super powerful."

4

One wishes Wendy and her father had experienced a rapprochement after that—or a détente *au moin*—but things quickly went from bad to worse. A mere three weeks later, the President declared war on Zambia, based on his suspicion that the Zambian president had subsidized the Terrible Event. As justifications for invasions go, it was pretty flimsy, but Wendy suspected the real justification was even flimsier. She suspected her father had set his sights on Zambia because it began with the letters "Za." Plus she'd heard the Interested Businessman whisper to him that it was very rich in gold. Yes, she was pretty sure now that the President was planning to go right through the nations of the world in reverse alphabetical order, making war and doing business. It would take the American People a little time to catch on because he was going backwards, but by then the invasions would have taken on their own inexorable logic.

To test her theory, one day she asked out loud if Yemen was next on the list of countries to be invaded. The Interested Businessman leaned over and murmured something in her father's ear and he got up from his chair and personally escorted her from the War Room. Everyone looked on in sympathy—sympathy for her father, not Wendy. The last thing you need to be dealing with when you're trying to make the world safe for democracy is a loud-mouthed teenage daughter.

Now banished from the Bunker, she wandered aimlessly through the White House, often coming to rest on the Solarium window seat. Sometimes she found her mother sitting there lost in thought, an empty watering can on her lap, but usually she had the place all to herself. The nicest thing about the Solarium, she'd decided, besides the light and the solitude, was that it put you eye level with the birds that congregated on the roof outside. They were nothing special—a choppy grey-brown sea of pigeons and sparrows, but she found them soothing to watch. All day long, they came and went as they pleased, their landings and takeoffs unremarked. What must it feel like to be that free? she wondered. What if *she* were to exercise her God-given right not to think about other people's pain—to act in her own self-interest, as the western congressman had put it? What if she were to follow her own heart's desire—where would it lead? Yes, that's right, the First Daughter was planning her escape. Spring had come to the nation's capital, and with it, her best shot at getting out of the White House.

One morning she went to see Duke O'Brian, the Director of the Secret Service, in his office. "Hey Mr. O'Brian," she said casually. "I noticed from the solarium window that the cherry trees are blooming. Do you think I could go to the Cherry Blossom Festival down on the Tidal Basin?"

"No," O'Brian responded without looking up from his computer screen.

"But isn't it important for us to act like it's business as usual?"

O'Brian folded his arms and sat back in his chair. "It's not business as usual."

"Look at it this way: if I don't get to see the cherry blossoms this year, the bad guys win."

O'Brian leaned forward to pick up a pen, then put it back down again. She was getting under his skin, she could tell. "Come on," she wheedled. "Don't you think it would reassure the American People to see me out at a festival?"

"Maybe," O'Brian conceded.

"Of course, if you don't think your men can handle it—"

"My men can handle it."

"No, I mean, really—"

"My men can handle it," he said through clenched teeth, and that was it, she was going to the festival. And further than that, if all went according to plan. She ran upstairs and stuffed a hoodie, some underwear and all the cash she had into a little backpack, and that was it, she was ready.

But these things are never easy. Just as she was heading out the front door with double her usual-sized detail, the First Lady came running upstairs from the Bunker. "Darling, where are you going?" she cried.

"Oh, to the Cherry Blossom Festival," she said, trying to sound nonchalant.

"I want to go with you!" her mother said, grabbing her hand, but to Wendy's relief, the agents said they weren't authorized to take her.

"Besides, Mom, you like roses, not cherry blossoms," she said kindly.

That made the First Lady cry, or perhaps she knew on some cellular level that her daughter was running away, because she clasped her to her bosom and wouldn't let go.

"I'm not a bad mother!" she sobbed. "I've been a good wife!"

"I know, Mom, I know," Wendy mumbled into the First Lady's sweater set. "I just want to get out of the house."

Finally, her mother released her. "I don't know why I'm so emotional!" she cried, looking around at the agents.

"No need to worry, ma'am," one of them replied stolidly. "She'll be back before nightfall." The First Lady nodded weakly and returned to the Bunker, wiping away her tears.

Wendy's first order of business upon arriving at the Cherry Blossom Festival was to take the Secret Service some place boring and educational so they'd start fooling around and forget to watch her again. To that end, she headed straight for the festival history tent. Luckily there was no one else in there, so her bodyguards took up positions around the outside perimeter and sent one of their number on a mission to buy fried dough.

She actually learned a lot about the Tidal Basin cherry trees while waiting to make her escape. Not many people know it was First Lady Helen Herron Taft's idea to plant them, nor that in 1910 she enlisted the help of Dr. Yokichi Takamine, a famous Japanese businessman, botanist and poet who had once visited the White House. Wendy spent some time musing over their correspondence:

Dear Honorable First Lady Helen Herron Taft:
How happy I am that you wrote to me! I remember with enormous pleasure my visit to the White House, especially the short time I spent alone with you in the Solarium, admiring your home plantings. And I think it is a wonderful idea, to bring the cherry blossom to America. I hope you will accept my gift to the American People of two thousand strong young cherry trees.
Yokichi Takamine

Dear Dr. Takamine:
I, too, enjoyed the time we spent together in the Solarium. I often think of that afternoon, and can imagine no greater honor than to accept your trees on behalf of the American People. What a lovely surprise!
Mrs. Helen Taft

Dear Honorable First Lady Helen Herron Taft:
Two thousand cherry trees sail to you today across the Pacific Ocean. There are many rituals associated with the blooming of the cherry trees in Japan, but my favorite is yozakura, or cherry blossom of night, when we view the flowers by candlelight. How I look forward to practicing this ritual with you on my next visit! And President Taft and the American People.
Yokichi Takamine

Dear Dr. Takamine:
The trees arrived yesterday, but I regret to say that an inspection team for the Department of Agriculture has informed us they are riddled with pests and diseases and President Taft has ordered them burned to protect American farmers. He seems to think this shipment of diseased trees was somehow deliberate on your part. I beg you, please write to assure him that was not the case, so that good relations between our two countries might continue.
Mrs. Helen Taft

Dear First Lady Helen Herron Taft:
How I suffered when I learned the trees had arrived in such a condition! In my heart, I felt a sakura fubuki, or cherry blossom storm, as when the wind scatters the cherry petals like snow. I put another two thousand healthy young cherry trees on a steamship this morning.
Yokichi Takamine

Dear Dr. Takamine:
I must confess your reply was a bit flowery for my husband's taste, but I managed to convince him that all is well, and we eagerly await the new trees.
Mrs. Helen Taft

Dear Konohanskuyahime:
May I call you this? It means "the goddess who can revive dead blooms." I am very happy that you accept my offer of another two thousand trees, and the planting will go ahead as planned. Why two thousand? You have never asked, but I wish to tell you: in remembrance of the breaths I took with you in the White House Solarium, which also numbered two thousand. I counted.
Yokichi

Dear Dr. Takamine:
Konohanskuyahime is a lovely name, but I think plain old Mrs. Taft will do just fine, as that is who I am, plain old Mrs. Taft, a married woman with three growing children. The new saplings arrived in excellent health and are being

*planted as I write this letter. Thank you again, on behalf of President Taft and
the American People.*
Mrs. Taft

Dear Mrs. Taft:
*How glad I am that Washington will soon be pink with blossoms! But I cannot
help mourning already the sakura chiru, when the cherry tree ends its blooming.
Such a short time to drink in so much beauty!*
Yokichi

Dear Dr. Takamine:
Yes, joy is fleeting, but you know that all too well, being a Buddhist.
Mrs. Taft

Dear Mrs. Taft:
*I know you are an honorable woman, but if I may be so bold: Have you ever
considered leaving President Taft and the American People, perhaps to make
your home abroad?*
Yokichi

Dear, Dear Dr. Takamine:
*I'm afraid that is impossible, but I shall never forget your kindness! Today, in
the nation's capital, and every year from now on, sakura saku. A million cherry
blossoms bloom!*
Mrs. Taft

It took a while to read all of that, and by the time Wendy peered out
of the tent her bodyguards were clustered near the entrance licking
powdered sugar from their fingers and talking about baseball. Seizing
the moment, she quickly crossed to the other side, lifted up the flap
and looked out at the Tidal Basin. The cherry tree branches hung low
to the ground, creating a thick canopy of pink and white flowers along
the rim of the basin, which she was hoping would completely hide
her from view once she passed through it. She ducked under the flap

and ran through the trees to the basin, then took off her shoes and scampered down the sun-warmed concrete bank, waving goodbye to FDR, MLK and Jefferson as she passed their stony shrines.

Her bodyguards didn't even realize she was missing for another half an hour, at which point they cleared out the festival and started hacking through the trees. It was a beautiful *sabura fubuki*, but by then the First Daughter was long gone.

Sir:
Your daughter's missing. Please advise.
Duke

WHAT? WHAT DO YOU MEAN MISSING? WAS IT AN ACT OF TERROR?

Sir:
It depends how you define "act of terror." We think she ran away.
Duke

DUKE I DON'T HAVE TIME FOR THIS! WE'RE INVADING YEMEN TODAY.

Sir:
My men are on it. Permission to classify her as an Enemy Combatant?
Duke

PERMISSION GRANTED. WAIT, WHAT? NO!
Sir:
Yes, sir. Permission to classify her as an Unprivileged Belligerent?

DUKE, SHE'S MY DAUGHTER.

Sir:

Yes, sir, your daughter, sir. But by law the Secret Service is required to protect her until she's twenty-one, so technically, she is a fugitive. Permission to proceed with Operation Retrieve Ingrate?
Duke

OH ALRIGHT, BUT HURRY UP! AND DON'T LET HER MOTHER KNOW SHE'S MISSING. I'LL NEVER HEAR THE END OF IT.

Sir:
How can we keep this from the First Lady? Please advise.
Duke

YOU'RE THE SECRET SERVICE! CAN'T YOU KEEP A SECRET?

Sir:
Permission to wiretap the nation? Permission to read everybody's emails?
Duke

SLOW DOWN, DUKE. ONE THING AT A TIME.

The President stuck his note to O'Brian into his top secret outbox with a chuckle. Duke O'Brian had his flaws, but you couldn't fault his conviction. He believed in what he was doing, and he believed in what the President was doing, too. Right after the Terrible Event, he'd come to the Oval Office to pledge his undying support. "If you want a glimpse of the future," the President remembered him saying, "picture a boot stomping on a face—over and over again."

He'd been hungry for O'Brian's certainty at that moment, dying to taste it, to know what it felt like to be a true believer. Unlike the President, O'Brian was a military man, and he knew how to draw the line between good and evil. He lived to draw that line. Oh sure, he was a bit like a big dumb dog, a big dumb dog who swims out to save you and ends up pushing you under the water with his big dumb paws, but he knew his job, which was the President's job now too: keeping the right people in and the wrong people out.

Except it was a little more complicated for the President, which was something O'Brian couldn't seem to get through his head, no matter how often he reminded him. The President of the United States isn't a goddamn security guard; he has Interested Businessmen to contend with plus the Press and the American People—and on top of all that, elections! But O'Brian had a solution for that, too: "President for Life!" he'd insisted after the Terrible Event. "You've got to make yourself President for Life!"

"Isn't that sort of—incompatible with democracy?" the President responded weakly.

"Nonsense!" O'Brian scoffed. "You're trying to protect democracy! But you need time."

The President sighed. At least O'Brian understood the gravity of the situation, unlike Wendy. What was she thinking, to run away at a time like this? Who knew who she might be talking to out there, or what she might be saying? He'd really had enough—he was too close to becoming a president-who-mattered to put up with her antics any more. I mean, did she have any idea what it would mean for the United States to become *the very first country to invade the entire world?* Oh sure, the U.S. had been invading other countries for a long time covertly—but nothing on this scale, nothing this out in the open. He reveled in the sheer perfection of his plan, which was going to earn him a nice little chapter in the history books. Actually, when you thought about it, there wouldn't really be any history after him, or politics either—only everlasting empire, like the Kingdom of God. The President looked around the empty War Room guiltily, because he didn't aspire to be—you know. That's the sort of thing that gets you into trouble.

But anyway, here he was, pretty much the biggest alpha male of all time—the Alpha and Omega Male, you might even say—and he couldn't control his own daughter. "The hell with it!" he muttered.

Nice guys finished last, and so did indulgent fathers. Pulling the note to O'Brian out of his outbox, he crossed out, SLOW DOWN DUKE ONE THING AT A TIME, and wrote in, GO FOR IT O'BRIAN.

Later that day, the First Lady's nerve endings began to tingle, and then to fray, until finally she stumbled into the War Room where the President sat ceaselessly scanning his awesome new digital map of the world. Not long after removing Wendy from the War Room, he'd banished everyone else, too, except by appointment. Only the Interested Businessman continued to come and go as he pleased.

"Where is she?" the First Lady cried as she entered the room. "What have you done with her?"

The President had planned to play dumb when this moment came, but his patience was wearing thin. "I didn't do anything with her," he snapped, keeping his eyes on the screen. "She ran away."

The First Lady collapsed into a chair. "Ran away?"

"Don't worry, the Secret Service is on top of it."

"But why?"

"Because they're legally required to protect her until she's twenty-one."

"No, why did she run away?"

The President shrugged. A nest of little red dots popped up on the screen—a new set of skirmishes—and he zoomed in, trying to pinpoint the locations.

Meanwhile, the First Lady was staring at her wavering reflection in the conference table's polished surface. Who is this man, she wondered, and how could I have married him? He wasn't always like this, was he? Once he cared about his daughter, didn't he? And me? And other things besides invasions?

But those other things seemed very far away at the moment. She took a deep breath and squared her shoulders. "I'll find her myself," she said, walking toward the door. "You can rot in here for all I care."

The President reached under the table and pressed a button, automatically locking the door. "Where do you think you're going?"

"Open it," she said, twisting the handle.

"I forbid you to leave the White House."

The First Lady's jaw dropped. "You what?"

The President sighed and tried another tactic. After all, he needed her cooperation. "What are the American People going to think if you let on that she's gone? What kind of mother will you look like?"

The First Lady's chest deflated and her eyes filled with tears. "Terrible," she whispered. The President wasn't sure if she meant her or him, and he didn't really care. "Leave it to the professionals," he said tersely. "Go water your plants."

The Joint Chiefs of Staff knocked on the door for their appointment and the President buzzed them in, avoiding his wife's eyes. The First Lady slipped past them, a wraithlike figure, and wafted down the hall.

Truth be told, O'Brian and his men hadn't even started the search for Wendy yet. Remodeling the White House pool house to accommodate the America Safe and Secure headquarters had proved much too onerous and distracting. A brand new department, created by the President after the Terrible Event to coordinate national security, ASS had absorbed the Secret Service, Immigration, Customs, Border Patrol, the Coast Guard, the Animal and Plant Health Inspection Service and FEMA—which is a lot of agencies to fit under one pool house roof!

The day the President made his first visit to ASS headquarters, O'Brian happened to be testing out GOTCHA, a new pre-crime screening software, in the midst of all the dust and hammering. This program was revolutionary, he informed the President, it could spot a terrible person before he even did anything terrible, from his furtive movements, sweaty brow and flickering eyeballs. But oh, how embarrassing, when some goofy minion trained the camera on the President during the demo and the screen flashed red!

O'Brian saved the day by thrusting a joystick into the President's hand and allowing him to maneuver a surveillance drone through the Rose Garden and into the Oval Office. It perched on his desk, relaying images of yellowed top-secret memos still sitting there from the day of the Terrible Event, voicing quaint concerns about the rise in unemployment and failing peace talks in the Middle East.

"Awesome!" the President crowed, his first expression of unadulterated delight since said day. "What do you think it would take to attach a missile to this thing?"

O'Brian squinted down at the dog-sized drone. "Well, for starters it would have to be bigger."

"Then get the Pentagon to work something up pronto. You could use it to patrol the White House!"

O'Brian thought it over. For like a second. "You got it!" he said, snap-pointing at the President.

"My man!" the President snap-pointed back. "And by the way, have you brought my daughter in yet? My old lady won't stop hassling me."

O'Brian picked up the drone carefully, like a beloved pet, and tucked it under his arm. "No, but we're very close, sir," he lied. "Very close."

O'Brian's statement was truer than he knew, for at that very moment Wendy was sitting less than two miles away from the White House in Union Station, stranded by the Great Flood of New Orleans. The trip she'd been planning out West had already been delayed for two days, with no trains coming out of the South. So she sat in a coffee shop, eyes glued to the TV alongside everyone else, watching a family who'd been stranded out on their roof for hours. Well, they'd been watching them for hours, the family had been there for days. The floodwaters were up to the eaves and all around them, a great brown putrid lake stretching as far in the distance as the eye could see. The grandmother lay motionless on the roof wrapped in an American flag while her grandsons waved bed sheets at news helicopters flying past, but the helicopters never landed, only zoomed in to get a better shot, the shot everyone in the train station was watching.

The family on the roof was black and poor—as was everyone on TV right then except for the newscasters. It had to be the most black people and the most poor people ever to appear on American television at one time, which wasn't exactly an accomplishment, given the circumstances. Some of the customers coming into the coffee shop, the white, wealthy ones, couldn't believe what they were seeing. "This can't be happening in America!" they said loudly, to no one in particular. "It's outrageous! Where's the President? Where's the National Guard? Where's FEMA?" *They're down in the Bunker, planning foreign invasions with the Interested Businessman*, Wendy wanted to say, but she kept her mouth shut. The rest of the customers were silent too, glued to their seats by what they were seeing, the awful confirmation of their everyday fears: *You're on your own.*

Every now and then the cameras interrupted the horror show to zoom in on homegrown relief efforts: people piling into church vans or cars loaded with supplies and heading south on Highway 64, or jumping into fishing boats or pleasure boats and making their way into the city by water. The flooding was beyond their capacity to help, of course, they couldn't create a working infrastructure overnight, plus the authorities kept shutting down the highways and diverting aid shipments, but the will was there, just as it had been after the Terrible Event.

If the will is there, Wendy wondered, then why does pain always seem to turn into war and drowning into spectacle? She looked around at the people staring at the TV screen, then back at the family on the roof, the grandsons sitting with their heads in their hands now, the motionless grandmother still wrapped in her flag. And she felt again the urge to run, as fast and as far as her feet could take her.

The First Lady inspected her map of the West Wing and then marched resolutely down the darkened corridor. She hadn't been on the first floor of the White House in over a year, and found it eerily quiet after the slumber party atmosphere of the Bunker. The hairs on her arms and neck stood at attention as she strained to make out the sound of explosions, fighter jets, shouting mobs at the White House gates. But no, all was calm, and once her ears adjusted it was a relief to escape the close quarters of the Bunker, the incessant beeping and buzzing of surveillance technology and the acrid smell of coffee and fear.

She was on her way to find the Vice President, who'd retired to his office soon after she broke off their affair, unable to stand being around her anymore without being able to touch or speak to her, and unable to stand being around her husband, who'd transformed overnight from an affable airhead into a marauding psychopath. Since he'd gone back up to his office, the Vice President was always spoken of down in the Bunker in hushed tones, as if he'd died or been committed to a mental institution, and that's how she'd preferred to think of him too—otherwise her own longing was simply too great to bear. But now she was on her way to ask him for help.

"How have I never been here before?" she said breezily, poking her head in the door. Her goal was to keep things light and cordial, but when the Vice President swiveled around in his chair, her voice caught in her throat.

"Hello, Lauren," he said quietly.

"Hello, Joe."

The Vice President drank her in with his eyes. She stayed in the doorway, afraid of what might happen if she sat down on his leather sofa.

"I've come to ask you a favor," she said, looking around the room. His TV beamed in images of New Orleans evacuees scrambling out of a dinghy onto a freeway overpass. "It's about that, actually," she said, folding her arms and pointing with her chin. The effect was of nonchalance, though she was merely trying to hide her shaking hands.

"I don't own a life raft, if that's what you're after," he said, playing it equally cool.

"Sort of," the First Lady said, blushing. She took a deep breath. "Joe, as you're aware, my husband's kind of gone round the bend..."

"Kind of?"

"Oh, Joe!" she blurted out. She couldn't bear the coolness. "Wendy ran away!"

"What?" The Vice President's face was suddenly a warren of concern and love.

"And I can't get him to care that she's gone. I can't get him to care about anything but making war. But this terrible Flood . . . if we could just get him to care about that, it would be a start . . . if you give me the War Room combination, then maybe I could slip in there and tell him about what's happening down in New Orleans. I'm sure he doesn't know yet; no one even bothers to brief him about domestic affairs any more. But if he knew, how could he not be moved to act?"

The Vice President nodded, thinking it over.

"Please, Joe. He's the father of my child. I have to try to reach him!"

The Vice President froze. "Wait, you're asking me to save your marriage?"

The First Lady looked away, unable to meet his eyes. "Please, Joe," she whispered.

Moments later, she walked away from the Vice President's office with the combination to the War Room, as she'd always known she would. Of course he had to let her try to turn the President around, because otherwise he would be a schmuck, and the Vice President was no schmuck.

The First Lady descended into the Bunker like Persephone into the underworld, clutching the code in her hand. Picking her way through sleeping bags and cook stoves, at last she reached the War Room's blast-proof iron door and punched in the numbers. When she entered, the President was asleep on the conference table, ankles crossed and hands folded neatly across his chest. The room was dark except for the blinking red dots on the digital world map, which covered his face with a virtual impetigo. The First Lady turned on the light and picked up the TV remote.

The President sat up and regarded her sleepily. "Hello, Lauren," he mumbled, with hypnopompic sweetness.

The First Lady walked silently around the room turning on monitors, as images of a sunken city filled the room. "There's been a terrible flood," she said finally. "New Orleans is underwater and the people down there are getting desperate."

The President slid off the table and into a chair. He pointed to a huge crowd of people sitting in front of the convention center, baking in the sun. "What are they doing?"

"They're waiting to be evacuated. They've been waiting for two days."

He pointed to a body rolled in a blanket lying on a traffic island. "What's that?"

"What does it look like?"

The President shifted his attention back to his wife, who stood before the bank of televisions with eyes ablaze, as his daughter had stood once before. Now that's a good-looking woman, he thought idly, taking in the First Lady's elegant bone structure and forties movie star figure. It had been a while. He felt faint stirrings in a body part obscured by the conference table, and gazed down at it thoughtfully.

"Are you kidding me?" the First Lady said.

The President shrugged and turned back to the map, using his remote control to zero back in on the conflict zones. The stirrings ceased, which was fine with him. Better that way, really. He needed to concentrate. "I'm sure FEMA's on top of it," he yawned. "How did you get in here anyway?"

"The Vice President gave me the combination."

The President's eyebrows shot up. "He did, did he?" Suddenly the stirrings were back. "In exchange for what?"

The First Lady eyed him coldly. "Please. He's twice the man you'll ever be."

The President snorted. "More like one-half."

She gestured towards the TVs. "If you're not going to do anything about this, then we have nothing more to discuss."

"Fine." He turned back to his map. "And by the way, I'll be changing that combination."

"Fine!" And the First Lady exited the War Room for the last time, slamming the blast-proof iron door behind her with a mighty bang.

But the next morning the Vice President found her lying on the Solarium sofa with the shades drawn. "Lauren, what happened?"

"Nothing," she answered, in a muffled voice. "He won't lift a finger to help."

The Vice President crossed over to the windows and opened the shades. "Well you can't just lie here."

"Why not?" she said, blocking the sunlight with her palm.

He sat down on the window seat a few feet away from her. "You've got to get on with your life."

"Like you got on with yours?"

The Vice President cleared his throat. "Listen, it's bad news for the country that you couldn't get him to change course, but it could mean good things for us."

The First Lady bolted upright at the suggestion, setting her feet on the floor and yanking her skirt down over her knees.

"Lauren?"

"I am not going to be the first First Lady to leave the White House without the President," she snapped. "I have a legacy, too, you know, and it is not that!"

Now the Vice President could've responded, "Desperate times call for desperate measures." He could've said, "To thine own conscience be true" or even, "but a love like ours doesn't happen everyday!" He almost did say one or more of those things, but he stopped himself. He wasn't going to beg. And it was that act of restraint, and the slightly Bogartesque cast of his features in profile, that did the trick.

"Stay," she murmured as he got up to go, reaching for his hand. "Because afterwards, who knows?"

"After what?"

"The Presidency," she whispered.

The Vice President shook his head and strode boldly to the door. Then he closed it and came back. With a small reckless laugh, the First Lady flung the pillows off the sofa, making way for his long body, her burning desire.

Or that's how they experienced it anyway, and who's to say, just because they were in round middle age rather than sinewy youth, that's not the way it happened? Afterwards, the Vice President lay with his arm around the First Lady and pondered this very subject. I am the Vice President, he thought, and the First Lady is my lady. She's not my very first lady and I'm not her very first man, but who cares about that? It's as if the skins of our youth have been abraded and now we stand before each other as two bleeding, loving chunks of flesh. No, that doesn't sound quite right. We're like two weary farmers tilling the dung heap of life together . . . No, she won't like that either. We're like two sagging half-filled sacks of rice . . . no. The Vice President decided just to enjoy the feeling rather than try to put it into words.

Of course, he reminded himself, she cannot truly be my lady until she is no longer the First Lady and I am no longer the Vice President, but I think that will happen sooner than she does. And he concluded that even though technically they were on the wrong side of things, they were really on the right side.

The First Lady stirred, and murmured something into his neck. "What, darling?" he asked, brushing her hair away from her face.

"Who's going to stop him?" she moaned.

The Vice President was silent. Who indeed?

A moment later, she jumped up off the couch and started running around the room picking up her things. "We've got to find Wendy! If anyone can reach him, she can. Oh sure, he kicked her out of the War Room, too, but remember how he supported her ridiculous campaign to raise awareness of World Pain?"

"Well, I actually thought she was onto something there," the Vice President said.

"Then come on! Let's go find her."

"But what about the Secret Service? Aren't they hot on her trail?"

"Forget the Secret Service—they're in it for the wrong reasons. It's up to us."

At the sound of "us," the Vice President's already sizeable heart expanded till he thought it would burst from his chest, and he struggled into his pants and grabbed his shoes.

The President was trying to go over the plan for Vietnam, but he couldn't concentrate. His wife's visit had really gotten under his skin. Not the stuff about New Orleans, the way she'd talked about the Vice President. He was sure of it—that SOB who was screwing his wife! That, kumbaya-singing, rose-sniffing SOB was probably having her in every room of the White House—Green, Blue, who knows, maybe in the Oval Office on his desk, his goddamn Kennedy-replica desk!

The President didn't have time for this. He needed to be focused on the invasion, which wasn't going well—the Vietnamese had proven difficult to subdue yet again. What was it with those people? But he couldn't stop thinking about this other thing, this thing between his wife and the Vice President. He was going crazy thinking about it, picturing their antics, imagining their conversations or lack thereof. It was as if he were being screwed by the VP. Here he was, sitting on the pinnacle of power, and that goddamn loser was screwing him to the goddamn wall.

How could she do this to him? What was it she'd said? He's twice the man you'll ever be. So disrespectful. So cruel. Wasn't he trying to make the world safe for democracy? For her? For their daughter? It kind of made him crazy, the way they treated him, but he couldn't let on how bad it felt. He wasn't going to give his wife the satisfaction. Because it wasn't about her, really. It was about—honor. Obviously, she no longer had any, but he was an honorable man.

He had to get the Secret Service involved. Maybe if they were performing round the clock surveillance on those two miscreants, he could put them out of his mind. Wait for the report, wait for proof, then issue his verdict. This had all gone on long enough, it was getting out of hand. He needed his daughter back, he needed his wife back, if only to torture her with recriminations. He needed to pick up his pieces, like in that Willie Nelson song—he was falling apart. He needed Duke. Duke would help him. Duke would fetch his pieces.

Wendy rubbed her eyes and drank the dregs of her fourteenth cup of coffee. She had a decision to make. The trains were up and running again—into and out of the South, which meant she still could get on that train to California. She could still go West, and going west would mean the same thing it had meant to that old congressman: the freedom to do what she wanted, to look out for her own damn interests, to run from pain—her own and the pain of others. Or she could take a train down to New Orleans. She could run toward the pain and try to stop it.

And of course, she had one more option: she could walk the half hour back to the White House and resume the mantle of First Daughter. She could worm her way back into the War Room, wriggle in between the Interested Businessman and her father, try to exploit his joy at her prodigal return to get more federal dollars for New Orleans. Plus she could see her mother again—she worried about her in that big white loveless house.

Wendy crumpled up her last coffee cup and threw it in the trash. As she left the café, the TV was still on, but New Orleans was no longer in the news.

O'Brian and the President sit in ASS headquarters watching the drone zoom around the White House grounds with a sweet little missile on its back. It's really a thing of beauty, the President thinks, plus it's so fun! He has his hand on the joystick, he's feeling good. O'Brian is on the job now, thankfully; he has his back. No mealy-mouthed sidekick is going to make his president look bad.

Can we call it kismet, that the First Lady and the Vice President should be the first moving targets to appear on that screen at the very moment the President is taking the drone out for a spin? The President would probably call it karma, but as we've seen, his perspective's a little skewed. Kismet or karma, it's a pretty volatile situation. Even O'Brian can see that. "Steady," he warns the President, but the President is almost too steady. He watches their movements with an icy calm.

The First Lady and the Vice President look up at the drone. They've been walking briskly across the North Lawn, but now they begin to run. They're holding hands, which pisses the President off. They're holding hands and heading for the northeast exit.

"O'Brian, I think there's been a security breach," he says quietly.

"Uh, sir? It looks like the First Lady and the Vice President."

"There's been a security breach, O'Brian," the President repeats. "You catch my drift?"

"Copy, sir," O'Brien murmurs uneasily.

Lauren and Joe are running flat out now—they've almost reached the gate. They look back over their shoulders, wide-eyed, as the President slams the joystick forward and accelerates, his thumb hovering over the button.

The First Daughter's sitting on a train to New Orleans, staring out the window at the kudzu-lined landscape and thinking about all the things she could care about and all of the ways she could show that care, now that she's left the White House. She could join a church group down in New Orleans, or the Red Cross, or an anarchist cell; she could become a deacon, a medic, a comrade. Who knows, from New Orleans she might go on to become a baker, a farmer, a bee-keeper; a doctor, a nurse, a mother. She could care about old people, she could work in an old folks home, she could care about kids. She could put a pre-school inside of an old folks home—what a great idea—joining little smooth plump hands with thin gnarled grasping ones. She could care about books, music, and movies now. She could care about art. She could care about history—the history of slavery, for instance, and how it drags on and on. She could care about science, about finding cures. She could care about drought. She could care about poetry. She could care about kite flying, sand crabs, the color orange. She could join with a few caring others to try to make a difference in the world; she could live with them in a commune. Or she could care for just one someone: a bearded young man on a bicycle, a smooth-faced woman on a Harley, a clumsy little girl with a lazy eye. She could care for a small house in the middle of nowhere with an avocado tree in the backyard. From now on, she would just be one person caring among billions of others, not spearheading a cause. But she'd be caring in her own particular way.

She still cares about her mother, and worries about her, but she knows she's going to be okay. Those nerve endings go both ways. She even cares about her father. Fortunately, or unfortunately, you don't stop caring about your father just because he's become a tyrant. But she no longer has to follow him from alpha to omega—or omega to alpha, as the case may be—she can follow her own bleeding heart wherever it takes her. And this, she's come to understand, is another kind of freedom.

END

Acknowledgements

My profound thanks to Andrew Sullivan and John Gosslee of C & R Press for their generous and unflagging support, and to Andrew for his keen edits. This book benefited greatly from the insights and energies of Danzy Senna, Maggie Nelson and Peter Gadol; my coworkers and students at CalArts; the Northeast LA Babysitting Co-op; the "Ken Train"; and the Sarbanes, Pappas and Moochnek-Ehrlich families.

Earlier versions of stories in this collection appeared previously in journals, and I'm grateful to their editors: "Laika Hears the Music of the Spheres" in *Entropy;* "Rosie the Ruminant" in *North Dakota Quarterly;* and "Who Will Sit With Maman?" in *P-Queue.* Excerpts from *The First Daughter Finds Her Way* appeared in *Merge* and *The Noulipan Analects.* The list of the world's peoples draws from Fiona Jack's *Missing Peoples, A Supplement to Merriam-Webster's Collegiate Dictionary, Eleventh Edition.*

OTHER C&R PRESS TITLES

FICTION

Spectrum
by Martin Ott

That Man in Our Lives
by Xu Xi

A History of the Cat In Nine Chapters or Less
by Anis Shivani

SHORT FICTION

Notes From the Mother Tongue
by An Tran

The Protester Has Been Released
by Janet Sarbanes

ESSAY AND CREATIVE NONFICTION

While You Were Gone
by Sybil Baker

Je suis l'autre: Essays and Interrogations
by Kristina Marie Darling

Death of Art
by Chris Campanioni

POETRY

Imagine Not Drowning
by Kelli Allen

Collected Lies and Love Poems
by John Reed

Tall as You are Tall Between Them
by Annie Christain

The Couple Who Fell to Earth
by Michelle Bitting

ANTHOLOGY

Zombies, Aliens, Cyborgs and the Ongoing Apocolypse
by Travis Denton and Katie Chaple

CHAPBOOKS

Notes from the Negro Side of the Moon
by Earl Braggs

A Hunger Called Music: A Verse History in Black Music
by Meredith Nnoka

CPSIA information can be obtained
at www.ICGtesting.com
Printed in the USA
FSOW01n1947230517
34353FS

9 781936 196654